MW00985713

DISCARD
HAMILTON PUBLIC LIBRARY

The Prisoner of
LIMNOS

The Prisoner of
LIMNOS

A FANTASY NOVELLA
IN THE WORLD
OF THE FIVE GODS

Lois McMaster Bujold

SUBTERRANEAN PRESS 2019

The Prisoner of Limnos Copyright © 2017
by Lois McMaster Bujold.
All rights reserved.

Dust jacket illustration Copyright © 2019 by Lauren Saint-Onge.
All rights reserved.

Interior design Copyright © 2019 by Desert Isle Design, LLC.
All rights reserved.

First Hardcover Edition

ISBN
978-1-59606-884-1

Subterranean Press
PO Box 190106
Burton, MI 48519

subterraneanpress.com

Manufactured in the United States of America.

I

---

*T*HE BOOKROOM IN the duke of Orbas's palace at Vilnoc was a lovely chamber. The spacious octagon, lined with shelves for scrolls and codices, was capped by a glassed roof. A well of good light for reading fell upon the central table where Penric sat. The quietude smelled of ink and paper, time and thought. It was his own failing that he couldn't concentrate upon a single word of the rare scroll rolled open in front of him.

He sighed and pulled the letter from the inner pocket of his white tunic, unfolded and read it once more. It had been handed to him this morning by the superior of the Bastard's Order here in Vilnoc. So, did he hope its contents might have changed since then? The lines penned by his own master the Archdivine of Adria, across the sea in Lodi, were quite short. And tart. And ordered him, for the third time—given that his mission to secure General Arisaydia for Adria had plainly failed—to stop loitering in Orbas and remove himself forthwith back to Lodi and his Temple duties waiting there.

Penric had written three temporizing missives to this high prelate, suggesting variously plausible reasons why he might linger in Vilnoc or even be assigned some ongoing diplomatic duty in the court of Orbas. All had fallen flat. At no point had he let slip his real reason for delaying, as that, he was sure, would have been even less well-received.

Nikys.

Or, more formally, the widowed Madame Khatai, sister to the young general and presently taking up new duties as lady-in-waiting to the duke of Orbas's daughter. Duties, she had repeatedly made clear to Penric, that left her no time for dallying. Nor dalliance. Or at least none with him.

Who knew what other courtiers about the palace might catch her eye? Or vice versa, definitely that. The widow had only her plump beauty for dowry right now, making her more a target for idle flirtation than courtship, though either vision was equally maddening. Even the dubious protection of poverty wouldn't last. The refugee siblings had arrived at the duke's court with no more than the clothes they stood in, but the general, already dispatched in the duke's service, would not long remain penniless.

Oh, she's still interested in you, Desdemona countered these glum musings.

So you claim, he thought back. *But I can't see it.*

The two-hundred-year-old Temple demon who lived inside of Penric and gave him the powers of a sorcerer was deeply imprinted by the lives of the ten women who had held her before him. He usually imagined this gave him a hidden advantage when dealing with females, but it seemed to be failing in this case.

You're too impatient, Des chided him.

You're too old, he thought back, grumpily. And not very prudently, but there was no concealing his thoughts from Des. *You don't remember what it's like.*

I promise I remember far more than you do, she shot back. It was all too likely. *Grant you, we've not seen this dance from inside the fellow's angle of view before. Though it appears to be equally absurd.*

Patient, impatient, hopeful or hopeless, certainly absurd, his pining scarcely mattered if he was going to have to bundle it all up and throw it overboard from some departing ship tomorrow. He might as well throw himself into the sea as well, and be done with it.

Now you're just being melodramatic.

Bah, leave me to brood in peace. He tried once more to bring his mind to bear upon the antique Cedonian prose laid out before him.

He should probably be packing. Not that the task would take long, since he, too, had arrived in Orbas with little more than what he wore—apart from his medical case and the folded-up costume of an auburn-tressed courtesan named Mira. Sora Mira, whose cleverness and professional skills had slid them all through the final set of dangers before they'd reached the safety of the border. Mira had been his demon's fifth possessor, a century past. He touched his hair. The last of the henna was almost out of his pale blond queue by now, but Nikys was not yet over Mira.

Not yet? Or not ever?

Desdemona, in all her complexity, was going to be a part of him until the day he died. As a Temple divine, he had a duty to care for his chaos demon; it had been made very clear in his seminary training that all their actions had to be ultimately his responsibility. But he was now beneficiary of two centuries of experience accumulated from ten wildly varied lives. (Twelve, counting the lioness and the mare.) To deny it all was beginning to feel like denying himself.

Which was not the same thing as keeping the direst bits private, true. Any man did that.

Agh. He gritted his teeth and reset the weights that held the scroll open.

At the scuff of sandals and a soft knock at the doorjamb, Penric looked up from his manuscript. As if summoned from his own thoughts like an apparition, although magic only worked that way in tales, Nikys stood in the entry to the bookroom. Penric kept his breathing level with an effort.

She was dressed for her day's duties in the Cedonian version of a sober summer gown, a loose linen dress belted at the waist, sleeves gathered in folds. It was dyed a widow's dark green that had lost its saturation to wear and washings and faded to an ambiguous sea-color. All hasty hand-me-downs from other ladies of the court, just as Penric's own white tunic and trousers were borrowings from the chapterhouse of the Bastard's Order, where he was also lent a room.

Her black curls were gathered by embroidered bands, holding them off her neck. Her dark eyes were as sober as her garb. She clutched a paper in her hand.

"Learned Penric."

His formal title that she'd used since their arrival in Orbas had replaced the *Pen!* she'd come to call him in their flight across half of Cedonia, and it felt like a slap. Rising politely to his feet, he retaliated in kind: "Madame Khatai. How may I help you?"

She cast him a distraught look, as if his question were not a rhetorical pleasantry, but some toweringly difficult puzzle. His heart perked up in curiosity.

"I just received this letter." She waved the paper and hurried across the bookroom to his side. "Really it was addressed to Adelis, but before he left he made me his executor for all his interests in his absence."

Those were duties she'd held before for her military brother. Given the hazards of his trade, it could all too easily turn into an executorship in fact, and it was a sign of his trust in his twin.

"It concerns me as much or more," she went on, "even though it's plain he's the real target." She bit her

lip and thrust the single page at him, obviously mean-
ing him to read it, too. By its cleanliness, it must have
arrived wrapped in some outer protecting envelope.

He took it, readily suppressing any faint qualm
that perhaps he should not be reading General
Adelis Arisaydia's personal correspondence. Or his
official correspondence, either.

It was in a spidery but clear handwriting,
unsigned and unaddressed unless that salutation, *To
the one of the yellow roses* meant more to Nikys than
to Pen. It went on: *You need to know that on the
second night of the full moon*—a scant week ago—*the
dam of your cradle-mate was brought to the spring on
Limnos by the order of the one who served you pickles. She is guarded there by his servants. The purpose
being plain enough, it is hoped this may reach you in
advance of any surprise, if the rumors of your destination prove true.*

*We will try to find out more. Yours in haste and
hope.*

"All right," said Pen. "I may read six languages,
but I need you to interpret this."

She ducked her chin. "I recognize the handwriting. It's Lady Tanar's eunuch secretary, Master
Bosha."

"And if I knew who either of these people were…?"

She waved an urgent hand. "Adelis was trying to court Lady Tanar two years ago, when we were both in Thasalon, before he was dispatched to thwart the Rusylli incursion. After which he was reassigned to the garrison in Patos, and after that, well, you saw all the disasters that overtook us there. In aid of his suit Adelis set me on to make friends with her, and we exchanged visits, oh, several times."

"So the yellow roses were, what, some courting gift from him?"

She nodded vigorously, making her bound-up curls bounce.

"I suppose it's a good sign that she remembered them two years later, but what about the rest of this?"

"*The one who served you pickles* has to refer to Minister Methani, who ordered Adelis be blinded with the boiling vinegar. Limnos is an island just off the coast near Thasalon—the Daughter's Order maintains a retreat there for high-born devotees who wish to withdraw from the world and dedicate their virginity to her. It also serves as a place for those who have grown old in her service to retire."

"Also the high-born ones, I would guess?"

"Not always, but certainly those who have risen high in Her Order. And also"—she took a deep breath—"as a delicate prison for noblewomen whom the emperor has taken hostage against their rebellious relatives. This says they've taken *my mother*."

Pen swallowed. "Oh."

"Oh, gods, I thought she would be safer than this. She's not Adelis's mother, after all, nor high-born. Most people don't know how close they are. Someone must have said too much to the wrong ears, at the imperial court."

"Unless this Methani fellow is clutching straws."

"Possible, but it hardly matters now."

Nikys and Adelis insisted they were twins, being born on the same day to two different mothers and the same father, on the grounds that had it been two fathers and the same mother, none would hesitate to dub them so. Old General Arisaydia's first marriage to a noblewoman with imperial connections had sadly been without issue for years, until he took a second wife, or concubine—Pen was a little unclear on Cedonian domestic legalities—and by whatever joke of the Mother and the Bastard, found himself with two offspring at once. Typically such women were expected to be rivals, but those two seemed to have united, instead, taking house together after the death of their husband in Nikys's late teens. According to Nikys, her mother had mourned the loss of the senior wife, a few years ago, even more than she'd mourned their husband.

It had all left Adelis's enemies at the imperial court with a dearth of potential hostages to hold against him, certainly.

"And what have the duchess or the duke to say to this?"

"I don't know yet. I came to you first."

Pen felt more alarmed than flattered. "Er, why?"

Her gaze upon him intensified. "You're a sorcerer. You smuggled Adelis and me out of Cedonia to Orbas. You escaped a *bottle dungeon*, and no one does that. I believe you could save my mother."

Penric gulped down his first impulse, which was to protest that those all had been flukes, unrepeatable. "We must take this to Duke Jurgo, to start. A threat against the loyalty of his new general concerns him closely, after all."

"Yes." Her hands clenched. "We have next to no resources, even between us, but he could help us if he chose."

Just exactly what she might have in mind, Pen shuddered to imagine. Perhaps Jurgo would be a voice of reason? Leaving the scroll open on the table, Pen folded and repocketed his own letter of the morning.

"What's that?" Nikys asked, seeing this.

"Oh"—Pen exhaled—"nothing of importance now. Let's go find Duke Jurgo."

They exited the bookroom together, Nikys's shorter steps for once outpacing Penric's leggy stride.

II

*T*HEY TRACKED THE duke, eventually, not to his cabinet but to the east end of the palace, where he was examining some renovations in progress. The work-crew foreman sent Nikys an unsolicited look of gratitude when she drew Jurgo off to a quieter courtyard.

Jurgo was a pleasantly ugly, mostly-affable man in his early forties, duke for some fifteen years and as solid in his position as possible for lord of such a beleaguered realm. Shrewd, or he wouldn't be so solid. If Nikys could present her needs as lying in line with his, she thought she might have a chance of gaining his support. At cross-purposes, she'd be weak indeed.

Jurgo settled on a shaded bench under the colonnade, Nikys standing stiff before him as he read her note. She strove to organize her thoughts through a head throbbing with more tension than since Adelis had been arrested back in Patos. And to shove aside, for the moment, a thousand thronging visions of what dire things might be happening to her mother *right now*. Women prisoners were almost never blinded, for example. Castration did not apply. The cutting-off of breasts, promising not only agony to the woman but starvation to her infant, was not usually threatened to women past childbearing. Retreats of the Daughter's Order did not feature dungeons.

Is she very frightened? Has she been cruelly treated? Nikys swallowed hard to keep control of her voice.

Penric leaned against a post and listened soberly as she again explained the strange message's import.

Jurgo tapped the paper in his hand, and asked, "Do you trust this? How certain are you of its senders?"

"Master Bosha's handwriting I know well, from other correspondence with Lady Tanar. Along with the roses, it's full of private things that Adelis would be expected to understand at once, just as I do."

"Not very full. It's quite short."

"The shorter, the better, for this sort of thing," Penric put in from the side. "Every unneeded sentence is another chance for betrayal, should it fall into the wrong hands on its journey."

Jurgo gave a conceding nod. "Could its writing have been bribed, or suborned?" His hand circled. "Compelled?"

"Lady Tanar Xarre is rich, and Master Bosha very loyal to her," said Nikys. "So not the first two. And I have trouble imagining any compulsion that would force him to write such a thing against her will."

Penric shrugged. "If he's a scribe, an offer to break his fingers might suffice. Or to blind him." While this was delivered in Penric's voice, the casual bloody-mindedness hinted it might be Desdemona talking.

It wasn't as if Nikys had spoken that much with Surakos Bosha, despite him being an ironic, watchful presence wherever Tanar went. So she couldn't *support* the conviction with which she said, "No." She added after a reluctant moment, "Although if someone threatened to break Tanar's fingers, it's hard to tell what might happen." Since *someone wouldn't live long* wasn't a thing she could say out loud. "But I can't picture how such an event might come about. Tanar is well-protected in her lady mother's household." Largely by Bosha himself, Nikys gathered.

"Even metaphorically?" asked Penric. "Pressure put on this Lady Tanar, her secretary writing to her dictation?"

Unhappily, Nikys turned out her hands. "To what end?" And hoped everyone else wasn't thinking the obvious, *Entrapment.*

The duke's canny eyes studied Nikys. "If General Arisaydia received this, as he apparently was intended to, what do you think he would do?"

Nikys hesitated.

Jurgo prodded, "Desert his post and attempt a rescue?"

"No."

"Lead his troops in some illicit sortie?"

"Never."

"How much would this impede his duties?"

"Not at all," said Nikys, both in simple honesty, and in aid of the duke's trust in his new general, "because he is Adelis. But he would be distracted and disturbed, as any man would."

"So no good could come from forwarding this to him."

"Except that he may find out from some less friendly source, at a worse time. Must, or what's the point of taking a hostage?"

"Hm."

"Unless," Nikys drew breath, "our mother was rescued already, and the report of that could come with it."

"I cannot lend troops for such a move, not against Cedonia."

"I know. I have a less costly and risky plan." At least, less costly or risky to Jurgo. "Allow me and Learned Penric to cross the border in secret and bring her out."

The duke glanced aside at Penric, whose mouth was set in a grim line, and did not scoff. "Wouldn't that just risk giving Adelis's enemies two hostages instead of one?"

Nikys demurred, "Given the weight of the first to him—to us—adding a second scarcely tilts the scale more."

"That risk could be averted," Penric said in a neutral tone, "by just sending me."

Nikys shook her head. "You don't know the country or the people, but I do. More to the point, they do not know you. This is too dangerous a business to expect them to trust some complete stranger." Of which Penric was one of the strangest. Although he could be convincing at need—she remembered that from Patos.

To Nikys's intense relief, neither man tried to gainsay this.

"So what is your scheme?" asked Jurgo, glancing between them.

"As far as I've come in an hour's thought," said Nikys, "Learned Penric and I could make our way much as we did before, passing ourselves off in whatever way seems best, to Lady Tanar's estate outside Thasalon. Take shelter and guidance there for the next step, that of getting on and then off the island with my mother. Repeat the stages in the opposite direction."

"Preferably better-funded this time," Penric put in. "Including a purse adequate for bribes. Still much cheaper than sending troops."

"Troops," Jurgo depressed this ploy, "were never an option. But the risk you'd bring to your proposed hosts seems beyond that invited by a mere friendly warning." He rattled the letter by way of emphasis.

"Yes," said Nikys, "and no. If Tanar is still considering my mother as her prospective mother-in-law."

"Was your brother's courtship prospering so much?"

"We'd hoped so. Before it was so brutally cut short."

"Mm, yes, that. The barriers between the general and the lady would seem insurmountable now." He touched his temple, and Nikys wondered if he was thinking of Adelis's disfigurement from the burn-scarring, as well as the new political divide.

"Now, certainly. But who knows what the future may bring?"

Jurgo didn't answer, and considering all the awful possibilities that might be a poor direction to bend his thoughts. He twisted in his seat to stare at Penric. "So are you volunteering, sorcerer? I thought you meant to go back to Adria."

"I must certainly report my actions to my Temple superiors," said Penric, glancing skyward as if to find those worthies there, "upon my return from Thasalon."

Jurgo smirked. "I see." He looked down at his sandals, looked up. "And here I thought you might have sought me out to report some happy news. That you had found reason to petition the Temple to allow you to stay in Orbas, for example." It was no secret that Jurgo had been wooing Learned Penric to join his ducal menagerie of scholars, writers, and artists, famous living ornaments to his court.

"That gift is not in my hands," said Penric, with a grave glance at Nikys. Implying that it was in hers?

Jurgo drummed his thick fingers upon his knee. "How soon would you imagine departing?"

"As soon as sensible preparation allows," said Nikys. "If there's one thing I've learned from my brother's military trade, it's that swift is better than slow." At once true, and another reminder of how valuable Adelis was to Jurgo.

Jurgo rubbed his lips, and Nikys hung suspended in the hot sunlight, watching his decision forming but unable to predict its direction. "Very well," said Jurgo at last. "Find my secretary Stobrek and work out the purse needed for the undertaking."

"*Thank you,* my lord," gasped Nikys, and would have fallen to her knees to kiss his ducal ring in wild relief, except he was already grunting to his feet, looking abstracted.

His look refocused on Penric. "Do you really think this can be done?"

"I..." Penric's teeth closed, fencing his reply.

"Let me rephrase that," said the duke. "Does Desdemona think it can be done?"

Penric's expression flickered from dismay to tranquility. "Yes, my lord. Or Ruchia does."

"...Ruchia? And which one was she, again?"

"The Temple divine who held Desdemona just before me. She was a scholar in her own right. And, er, an agent of my Order who completed many varied tasks, in the forty years of her career as a sorceress." Pen grimaced, and added, "Oh, just spit it out, Pen. She was a spy, and a good one, too."

That was Desdemona, without question.

Even Jurgo caught it, by the wry smile that turned his mouth. "Let us all hope so."

III

─────────────────────────────────────

*I*T WAS NOON the following day when Penric and
Nikys boarded a small private coach in Vilnoc
to make their way west. In this region it was less
than three hundred miles in a straight line from one
coast of the peninsula to the other, but even the Old
Cedonian military roads up through its former prov-
ince of Orbas were neither straight nor level. The
team was reduced from a smart trot to a laboring
pull on the upward slopes, and an even more careful
descent, wooden brakes screeching and smoking. It
was still vastly faster than walking, and more com-
fortable than mule-back. Much as tertiary fever
was better than plague, Pen reflected as the coach
bumped and rocked.

Pen shoved with his foot at his restocked medical case that had slid across the floor. Bringing it along had seemed prudent, even if the last thing he wished to do was practice medicine again.

Oh, you're beyond the need for practice by now, lad, murmured Des, in her acerb version of encouragement, and Pen let his tired lips twitch in thanks.

Nikys fussed with the few belongings they'd thought they could carry over the more rugged mountains when they made the turn north to slip over the border. Their boots and riding clothes for that part of the trek were packed away. For the coach, Nikys wore a belted dress, with a sort of loose surcoat flung over it for protection from the road dirt, which would have made a more convincing apron without its fine court embroidery. Pen had obtained a man's tunic and loose trousers of this country, the latter cuffed and buttoned at the ankle to hastily alter for his height. The simple cut left his status ambiguous, and told nothing of his calling.

Nikys was still strained in his presence, a tension seemingly made worse, not better, by her sudden need for him. He'd not seen her look so fraught since his first sight of her in the villa garden in

Patos, despairing over her unjustly blinded brother. She let the noise of the coach be an excuse for not attempting to talk, and Pen allowed it. He didn't think she'd slept at all last night, for after the first change of horses she leaned over in her seat and dozed despite the rattling.

Pen studied the horribly awkward angle of her neck, and slipped across to supply himself as a human pillow. She turned over and curled up with her head on his thigh, with a wheeze that he was pleased to take as gratitude. He let his hand slide over her torso to hold her secure, rewarded when she slipped into a deeper sleep. He alternated between staring out the window at the bony countryside, and regarding the unbony woman in his lap. Profoundly loyal she was, to those few she took as her own; her brother, her mother. Pen had no idea how he was ever to get himself on that short roster. By an effort doomed to be unappreciated, he kept his free hand from playing with her tumbled hair, black and shining as the best fresh ink.

When the coach halted at the next change and the sharp voices of the ostlers echoed outside, she stirred at last, with a sinuous stretch and an enchanting purring noise. She lay a moment in muddled relaxation, fingers clutching him like a real pillow; then, alas, her disordered world crashed back in upon her. She jerked upright with a yelp, clipping Pen's chin with her head in passing, and flinched to the other side of the seat.

"Ow," Pen complained mildly, rubbing his jaw. She stared at him a little wildly for a moment, and he added, "You fell asleep. Looked like you needed it."

"Oh," she said, partly regaining her composure. She rubbed her head in turn and managed an "Oh, sorry. Strange dream."

"No matter."

They both descended for the usual visit to the coaching inn's privy, a turn about the yard, and hastily quaffed purchased drinks, in this place beakers of over-watered wine. By the time they reboarded the vehicle, she'd put herself to rights again, seeming better for her nap.

"We've hardly had time to talk about how we are to explain ourselves to people," she said as they settled to endure the next stage. "I don't think we can pass as brother and sister." She glanced doubtfully across at his pale cool blondness, back to her own terracotta Cedonian warmth, and pulled straight a stray black lock, glancing up at it before letting it curl back. "Not even half-siblings. And I'd rather we weren't husband and wife."

"Yes," said Pen wryly, "you told me that once before."

She bit her lip, flushing. "You know what I mean."

"I do," he sighed. Teasing Nikys had its charms, but now was so clearly not the time. "Keep it simple, I expect. Don't say anything. People will make up their own explanations."

"So I fear," she murmured ruefully.

"You don't have to care, and they don't either. We're just passing through. While being your husband would give me an unassailable right to protect you, being your courier will serve in most cases." He hesitated. "As always, it's best not to mention my calling. To anyone. Not even to your friends, unless some urgent need arises." His sorcerer's Temple braids were hidden in the very bottom of his medical case, though he had brought no white robes. If it ever came to the valise being violently turned out, it was likely the assailant would be discovering Pen's abilities in more direct ways.

Penric contemplated the unknowns ahead of them. He'd studied the duke's maps last night, planning their route much more logically than their prior lurching flight, but what of all the human hazards?

"This Master Bosha you keep mentioning," he said slowly. "The castrate secretary. Is he a slave, then?" Both those Cedonian customs were alien to Pen's mountainous home country, a land of obstreperous small freeholders scraping out their livings from soil almost as rocky, though damper and colder, than Cedonia's.

"Very much not!" said Nikys, sounding surprised by the question. "Although he has been a servant of the Xarre family for a long time. Since Tanar was six, she once told me, and she's now twenty, so over fourteen years."

Pen did a little historical arithmetic. "That would have been about the year the present emperor took power." Bloodily, although that was the way in Thasalon as often as not. "Any connection?"

"I know nothing about Surakos Bosha's family background. It was a very disrupted year in the capital." Nikys frowned in thought. "I don't think he's low-born. He had a good education somewhere. There are hints he was once one of those men of good family who are cut by choice, to improve their chances of rising very high in the imperial bureaucracy."

Pen made an effort not to cross his legs. "That's more dedication to a career than I would have. Although there is a group of Temple singers in Lodi who have also freely chosen to be made castrates, consecrated to their craft and their god. Male sopranos. I've heard them sing twice, at festivals there. Hauntingly beautiful. I admit, I would not argue their calling with them." Because song, being a gift of the spirit, was considered a most acceptable offering to the gods.

Nikys nodded. "Some do that in Thasalon as well. I don't think that's what he came from, though. He's no soprano." She stared across at Pen in an unsettling manner. "I thought he was the strangest man I ever met, until I met you."

Pen cleared his throat, restraining himself from pursuing that comparison.

But Nikys went on unprompted. "He's still the palest, not even excepting you. He's a true albino. Like a white rabbit, or white horse."

A gelding, perhaps, murmured Des, all fake innocence. *I wonder who rides him?*

Tasteless, Des. Or had that been Mira? *Hush, I need to hear this.*

"His hair is pure white. At night his skin seems bleached like the moon, although it's rather pink in bright light. Which he avoids—he burns in the sun worse than you do." She frowned in speculation at Pen. "Do you suppose the people in your home country could be part albino?"

"Not as far as I know," said Pen. "Because real albinos do turn up, as rarities, I have heard, and they are considered just as odd there. If not as sunburned."

Pen tried to picture a man who would take up a tender trade as a wealthy young lady's private secretary. Plump, probably—he'd heard cut men were prone to run to fat as they aged—rabbity, maybe timid and twitchy. Odd. Well, he'd deal with the fellow when he came to him.

"What more can you tell me of Lady Tanar?" he went on. Because they would be wagering their lives, as well as their cause, upon her goodwill and power to aid them. "Should we be looking to her mother for command of resources? Did Lady Xarre favor Adelis's suit? Or would she thwart her daughter's dangerous charity, if she finds out?" This was no girls' prank they were engaged in, but something perilously close to treason. With all the gruesome Cedonian penalties that applied, if discovered.

Nikys pressed her lips together in disturbing doubt. "That's a decision I'd leave to Tanar. I've only met Lady Xarre the once. She's long widowed, and lives retired now, seldom leaving her estate. Doesn't dabble in the Thasalon court, even though she has the rank for it. I understand she's very active in ordering her financial affairs, through a troop of trusted retainers. She makes Tanar her apprentice in all her doings, since Tanar is her only heir, which seems to me very much more to the point than making her learn embroidery." Nikys paused as if to consider this. "Tanar thinks so, too."

"And did Adelis?"

"I don't think Adelis was quite aware of it, never having been a soldier's wife." As widowed Nikys once had been, aye? "But she would have been very well fitted for managing all the tasks of his own wide holdings." She scowled. "Before he was stripped of them." And then, "Our other mother—Adelis's lady mother—did such for our father."

Since all of Penric's worldly goods could fit on six mules, and had, this was not work he knew. He supposed it was much like his older brother Rolsch's duties back at Jurald Court, multiplied by several. Or several dozen, it sounded like.

Pen wondered if it would be better to route around these untrusted allies, and proceed directly to the island. Somehow.

Local knowledge is never to be scorned, murmured Des, or with luck Ruchia. *If not to be relied upon blindly, either.*

That was assuming Nikys's mother was actually on Limnos, and the whole thing not a trap from the beginning.

If it is a trap, said Des serenely, *it was made to fit Adelis. Not us.*

Des, it seemed, was much less terrified by this return to Cedonia than he was. Of course, a demon could not be killed, exactly. *Are you saying I would be a surprise?*

Oh, Pen. You have been a surprise from the beginning.

IV

HE DWINDLING LATE-SUMMER light ended their first day of travel much too soon, Nikys thought. Pushing on through the darkness on Orbas's difficult hill roads would be so slow as to not be worth it, Penric persuaded her, and they should not arrive at their hardest stretch over the border mountains already exhausted. What passed for coaching inns in Orbas were more primitive than those they'd encountered in Cedonia, and Penric in his role of her courier was hard-pressed to get her a private chamber, but Nikys scarcely cared. She'd have slept in the stable if she'd had to. They took the road again in the damp gray of dawn.

Even Penric was slow to come awake in the initial hour, but he soon glued himself to the window like the foreign sightseer he wasn't, asking questions about the passing countryside Nikys mostly couldn't answer. But when they'd resettled themselves in the coach after the first change, his boundless curiosity took another turn.

"Were both your mothers called Madame Arisaydia? Because I'd think that would be confusing." At her stare, he added, "In my country men only have one wife at a time. Officially, anyway. Although I suppose my mother and my sister-in-law shared out their name for some while before my mother died, and you were always having to clarify which one you meant."

"No," said Nikys. "Adelis's mother was Lady Arisaydia, or Lady Florina. Or Florie, to my father. Concubines keep their patronymics. So my mother was always Idrene Gardiki." *Is*, Nikys fiercely vowed. "Though my surname was Arisaydia, of course, before I was married." She frowned out the other window at the vexingly endless rocky hillsides. "My other brother was Gardiki for just a brief time before he was adopted by his grandmother's family, and after that he was Rodoa. Ikos Rodoa." She prayed he was well out of this. With luck, he'd be working somewhere on the far northern peninsula, and would not even have heard of their mother's arrest. This dangerous mess was much too far over his head for him to mix into.

A startled silence, then Pen said, "Who? What? I thought you and Adelis were the old general's only children."

"That's right." She glanced across at him, trying to decide if his expression was dismay or just surprise. "To be fair, I didn't know he existed either, till he came to my father's funeral. My mother never spoke of him because the separation had made her sad, she said, but when he reached his majority he could come on his own, and did. He visited us a few times after that, when his travels took him nearby. He's a master bridgebuilder, now, and goes to work all over Cedonia. For various towns, usually."

"Uh...older brother? Surely not younger. Was your mother a young widow, too?"

Nikys smiled. "Not exactly. Although only by ill-chance. She was actually the daughter of one of my father's senior officers. She fell in love with a junior officer. The way one does, I suppose." Nikys tried to remember if she'd ever been so smitten by the army lads at that age. She'd never been that carried away, to be sure. Firmly, she kept herself from glancing at Penric's long, blond, and entirely unmilitary elegance. "They meant to marry, or so she said. It likely would not have been opposed even though her family thought her too young, but he was ordered out suddenly to, gods, I don't even remember which clash she told me, and killed in the battle. He was the Rodoa family's only son—only surviving child, I believe—so when my mother turned out to be pregnant, they took her in. Except, although the grandmother desperately wanted the boy, she didn't really want my mother—they didn't even offer to make her a ghost bride."

"I don't know what that is." A short hesitation. "Oh, thank you, Des. They really do that?" He turned to Nikys. "Marry people to dead people?"

"Not often. It's a sort of adoption, as much as anything. If they'd had the ceremony—it's sometimes held at the graveside, but more often with a memori tablet—my mother would have become a daughter-in-law of the house. With certain rights of support and inheritance, among other things. Without that, she was used more as an unpaid servant. It was a very uncomfortable time for her, I gather. So after Ikos was weaned, and my father sent Lady Florina to convey his offer—really, their offer—my mother let herself be persuaded, even though it meant giving up her firstborn. Grandmother Rodoa was all for it, naturally."

Penric's face scrunched up as he wrapped his mind around this bit of family history. "It sounds complicated."

Nikys shrugged. "I suppose. But Ikos was why my father and Lady Florina became so interested in my mother—proof that she could bear children, which was what they both wanted. It all seemed to work out for everyone in the end, somehow. Certainly for me."

He smiled crookedly, giving a conceding nod. "An excellent result."

She tried not to be warmed by the compliment. She was *using* this man, this sorcerer, she reminded herself. She couldn't remember, in the chaos of the past two days, if she'd ever offered him any payment or reward for risking his life in this frightening venture. Even soldiers were paid, after all—quite insistent upon it if the army payroll was in arrears, as it so often was.

She dismissed her conscience, ruthlessly. She was ready to use anything and anyone to hand, if it would help her to carry out this rescue.

And thus what, exactly, was her ground for scorning his lewd use of Mira, or Mira's lewd use of him, to get them all past the border before?

The courtesan hadn't just been a costume, or a ploy. She was in some strange sense still alive, inside his crowded head. And always would be, along with the rest of her barely understood sisterhood. To convert Nikys's *I fear they know too much* to *I hope they know enough* had only taken one cryptic note.

She settled back with a sigh, willing the team to trot faster.

AT THE western end of the main road from Vilnoc, service for coaches terminated at the grubby garrison town that guarded the three-way border between Orbas, Cedonia, and Grabyat to the southwest. Adelis had passed through here just a few weeks ago with Jurgo's troop, in aid of the ally in that next realm. Nikys did not dare ask after him. Finding the army post and its commander, Nikys and Penric presented the sealed letter from the duke commanding all aid be given to them, which proved to be a sergeant, a muleteer, and four sturdy animals.

Another dawn start brought them, by dusk, to the broken spine of the last ridge between Orbas and Cedonia, where they camped for the night. Neither the sergeant nor his assistant asked any questions; Nikys gathered they were used often as guides to slip spies over the border.

"It's likely a regular business," murmured Penric. "You wonder if the empire uses the same route, or if they have their own favorite backdoor for their agents."

Adelis might have known.

Nikys could see why they'd waited for daylight for the next leg, emphasis on the leg as they were forced to dismount and lead the mules over the worst ledges. There was no breath left for conversation. They really couldn't have taken this route the other way three months ago, when Penric was still recovering from the injury to his heart; another point, Nikys grudgingly conceded, to Mira.

In the late afternoon, they paused in their equally rugged descent for the sergeant and the muleteer to scout ahead and be sure the military road, along which Imperial soldiers ran regular patrols, was temporarily unpeopled. It proved a bare cart-track. They skittered across, the muleteer coming behind to blot out their prints, and worked their way as quickly as possible down out of sight.

Nightfall brought them to a village where they could hire horses from an incurious farmer, whom Nikys thought likely a retired soldier, anyone's guess from which army. After the briefest introduction, with names notably absent, and the purchase of some grain, the sergeant, the muleteer, and their animals faded away into the darkness, not lingering to be seen and reported by less indifferent eyes. This time Nikys and Penric really slept the night in the stable, and were grateful for it.

Another long day's ride downhill brought them to the first good coach road north of the border, which ran on west to Thasalon. They dismissed their guide and his horses with a double fee, half for the mounts and half for the silence. A larger town and a busier inn allowed them to take two adjoining rooms, wash, and change into their next set of clothes and new personas.

After their late supper, Penric bade Nikys a polite goodnight and left her to lock the connecting door behind him. She sat staring numbly at it for a while, too exhausted to stand up after three solid days of grueling riding. This was, she realized, the first and possibly last time she would be alone with the sorcerer. With the man. The most wasted opportunity ever...

The coach-hire the next morning seemed to care only that their coin was good, which thanks to Jurgo's generous purse it was, and to get them on their way as efficiently and lucratively as possible. They would reach the hinterlands of Thasalon by sundown. Still unremarked.

While not having to stop and let Penric steal them funds from local temples was certainly a boon, this round, Nikys suspected the return journey might not run so smoothly.

V

---

*I*N THE MOONLESS shadows, Penric looked up and down the long wall that surrounded what Nikys claimed was the Xarre estate a few miles east of Thasalon. He hoped she was right in her identification; all the walls in this suburban area had looked alike to him. They'd dismissed their coach half a mile back, to conceal their destination from the curious postilion, and it had made a long, nervous trudge in the gloom.

He extended his hand to the lock on the postern gate, and thought, *Des.*

The heavy iron mechanism fell open to this well-practiced magic. Pen held the thick plank door ajar for Nikys, and she hoisted their luggage and slipped inside. Pen closed it as silently as possible after them.

Pen concealed their cases behind a healthy flowering bush, outlier of the extensive garden. "Can you see well enough not to trip?" he whispered.

"Not really," Nikys murmured back. He reached for her hand and led her off down the winding paths that were not dark to him.

There were supposed to be guards, she'd told him, if more like caretakers than soldiers, and dogs let loose at night. No sign of the first, but within minutes a pair of the second came bounding up, snarling. A quick tap of nerve-tweak stopped their alarm-barks, followed up barely soon enough by a brief shamanic geas to persuade them that these intruders were not enemies, but the best of friends. So they were slammed into not by an attack, but by an attack of sociability. Tails wagged like cudgels, thumping into Pen's thighs as the beasts swirled around them. A couple of haunches of beef might have worked as well as pacifiers, Pen thought, had he possessed them.

"These aren't dogs, they're *ponies*," gasped Pen, fighting for his balance.

"Mastiffs," nodded Nikys. "Ew, stop licking me, you huge thing!"

Pen fended off tongues the size of washing cloths, and a miasma of slime and dog-breath. With this unwanted, but at least silent, honor guard panting around them, they made their way to another long, blank wall, the exterior of the residence proper. In the usual Cedonian style, the manse was built around an inner court, giving a cold stone shoulder to the outside. But it was three floors high, and a lot larger than Pen was used to seeing. There were neither windows nor entries on this side of the ground floor, locked or no, but the stories above were pierced with a number of long doors opening onto wooden balconies. Golden candlelight filtered through a few of the delicate carved lattices.

Nikys squinted into the shadows and counted down the doors. "That one," she whispered, pointing up to one of the glowing screens. "Second floor."

The wall was entirely without handy ladders or climbing vines. "You do know my powers don't extend to flying, right?"

"You were a mountaineer. You said?" Her look up at him was far too expectant.

"I was younger. And lighter. And stupider." Nonetheless, he approached and studied the problem, mapping out the slight cracks and irregularities in the stuccoed surface. *Maybe*. Although a stone tossed up against the shutters might do to draw attention, he'd be happier to assure himself first it was the right attention.

"Could you stand on my shoulders to get a start up? You're not that heavy a man…"

Pen disliked this picture, but there seemed no other way. He had her brace against the wall, planning his leap to linger on this prop as briefly as possible. He took a deep breath and bounded, one, two—he could feel her straining body dip beneath his feet—and just caught one hand-grip on the balcony's edge. Then another. A foot-shove against the wall, alarming when a bit of old stucco gave way. Then heave *up* and over the balustrade.

He landed crouching as quietly as he could, then unfolded to tiptoe over and try to peek through the lattice. A well-appointed sitting room, it looked like, the scent of expensive beeswax candles, but he saw no identifiable figures.

He tapped cautiously on the carving. "Hello?"

Only Des allowed him to evade, narrowly, the silent thrust of a thin knife blade through the lattice.

He yelped, and yelped again as the door slammed open, bashing him hard in the nose. A swift figure,

a swirl of fabrics, and he was spun about. A wiry
arm snaked up through one of his own, yanking
back and immobilizing it, and the blade snapped to
his neck.

And stopped, although pressing alarmingly into
his skin. A hot huff of breath puffed against his ear.

Don't move! said Des, redundantly. *That blade
is poisoned!*

All of Penric's carefully rehearsed introductions
flew wide into the night, and he gasped out only,
"I'm with Nikys!"

A hesitation, thank the Bastard, though the
grip didn't slacken. "On your knees," came an edgy
tenor voice, sounding as sharp and dangerous as the
blade. "Face the light."

Pen descended at once, free hand going up palm-
out in surrender. Or prayer, either one just now. The
steel grasp released him. Quick steps circled him,
and Pen looked up past fine linen trousers and a
fall of an embroidered silk outer robe to a beard-
less, scowling face as pale as the absent moon. Thick
white hair was drawn back from the brow in some
queue or braid.

A female voice sounded from within the chamber: "Sura, what is it?"

"An intruder. It seems."

"Visitors, I assure you!" protested Pen.

"You pick an odd way of presenting yourself."

"We are on an odd errand."

The other leaf of the lattice swung open. "Stay inside, Lady Tanar!" the man commanded.

Ah, said Des. *At least we seem to be in the right place. Good.*

Disregarding this, the woman emerged. Slender, a little shorter than Nikys, also hung about with rich fabrics, loosed in the cooling late-summer night. She evaded the man's half-hearted attempt to strongarm her back within, instead tripping to the balcony rail and peering over into the shadows. "Nikys?"

"Tanar?"

"I thought you were in Orbas!"

"We were. We got your note to Adelis. And traveled as quickly as we could. Can you come and let me in before your dogs drown me in drool? We probably should not be seen before we can talk."

"Oh, dear. Stay there, I'll be right down."

Lady Tanar darted back inside. The white-haired man made a futile noise of protest, half jerking in her wake, but then turned back to guard his prisoner, the unknown threat. He'd recognized

Nikys's voice, apparently. Pen tried to feel reassured by that.

"Can I get up now?" he asked humbly.

The man thought about this for a moment. "Slowly."

Pen complied, entering the sitting chamber at his gesture. One pale hand made the knife disappear inside his robe, and the man rolled his shoulders, allowing his murderous air to dissipate.

He's carrying four blades concealed, Des reported. *And every one is poisoned*. She considered. *Drugged, anyway. They are not all the same.*

In the better light from the mirrored wall sconces, Pen could see the man's irises were a thin carmine; likely they showed pink when the pupil contracted in daylight. His pinched eyebrows, too, were white. His face was fine-boned and regular, if tense. An old scar puckered the left side of his mouth, giving an impression of a permanent smirk, belied just now by the downturned right. His snowy braided queue, tied off with colored silk, reached halfway to his waist.

My word, said Des. *That one's almost as pretty as you, Pen.*

Pen ignored this. But he bid a glum goodbye to his prior mental image of the pudgy, timid eunuch secretary, swapping it out for this overdressed white snake of an assassin standing taut before him. "Master Bosha, I presume?"

A short nod. "And who are you?"

"My name is Penric. I've taken the duties of Madame Khatai's courier for this journey."

"Do you know what this journey is in aid of?"

"Yes."

The carmine eyes narrowed. "I see." He reached into his robe—Pen tensed—but the manicured hand emerged holding only a fine cotton handkerchief. Ironed and scented. He handed it blandly across to Pen. "Don't drip on the carpet."

"Ah. Thank you." Pen mopped at his upper lip, wet with blood. His price for the shamanic compulsion on the dogs, but let Bosha assume it was from the violent encounter with the door; maybe he'd feel guilty. Likely it was the result of both. The cloth grew saturated before the trickle stopped, at about the same time the door onto the courtyard gallery opened and Lady Tanar slid through, followed by Nikys.

Nikys pressed her hand to her breast and sighed out relief as Tanar closed the door and locked it, as though they had reached a safe refuge after their arduous journey. Pen was not so confident.

Urgently, Tanar turned to Nikys. "How is Adelis? Where is Adelis? We heard he was blinded in Patos, and then we heard he'd turned up somehow in Orbas, and none of it made *sense*."

Nikys took a breath as if to answer this, but then looked imploringly at Penric.

He managed, "The seething vinegar was inadequately applied, and thanks to his sister's good nursing, he recovered his sight. As soon as that was apparent, he fled to Orbas to save the emperor's agents from coming back and trying again." The official story. That Penric had rebuilt the young general's half-boiled eyes with the most delicate and difficult week of uphill medical magics he had ever brought off was not something he wished to confide. Here or anywhere.

Nikys's mouth compressed in silent disagreement with this reticence, but she yielded to his tacit wishes. "Duke Jurgo employed Adelis at once, and has sent him off to command his expedition against the Rusylli incursion in Grabyat. Adelis having defeated the Rusylli once before, to no imperial thanks. I can only hope Jurgo will do him better. He could hardly do him worse."

Bosha's lopsided lip seemed to twist in a real smirk, contemplating the gratitude of princes. He stood back with his arms folded, his attention never straying far from Penric.

"Adelis was weeks gone by the time your note came to my hand," Nikys went on. "In exchange for not distracting him with the news, the duke supported Penric's and my journey to try to get our mother out of Cedonia, and then to Orbas with me. Somehow." She looked back and forth between Tanar and Bosha. "I don't know how much aid you can give without danger to yourselves, but whatever help you can spare, I beg it of you now."

"Of course!" cried Tanar, notably not seconded by Bosha. "You poor dear. All the way from Orbas, so swiftly? Here, you must be exhausted, come, sit. You should drink something." She looked more doubtfully at Penric. "You too, ah, Master Penric." A vague courtesy title, flattering if he were a mere servant. Pen didn't think she took him for a mere servant. But he followed Nikys to the small round table with chairs placed to the side of the room, suitable for two people to take a light repast. Bosha, without comment, set two more chairs around it, brought a carafe of sweet red wine and a pitcher of drinking water from a sideboard, and served out glass goblets of the mixture all around.

That's not poisoned, is it, Des? Pen asked in worry.

Not so far, she returned darkly. *I'll stand sentinel.*

Tanar touched her lips, and asked in a lower tone, "Was he terribly burned?"

Pen watched Nikys struggle not to answer with the truth, *Hideously.* "It was not good. He was in dreadful pain for a while. But the scars are healing mostly flat, and confined to the upper half of his face, and the redness is supposed to fade in time. Except for his eyes; they didn't come back brown. They are a kind of garnet color now. It unnerves people, but he says that's fine, given his profession."

Tanar's own gaze flicked to Bosha and away. "That's all right. I've always thought red was a lovely color for eyes."

Bosha spread his hand on his heart and offered her an ironic seated bow, which she dismissed with an amused quirk of her lips.

"And if he has already taken up a new command, he must have made an excellent recovery." She smiled in relief, sitting more upright.

"I thought it miraculous, myself," said Nikys, steadfastly.

No remark, Pen? murmured Des, preening a trifle. *Hush.*

Nikys turned more intently to Tanar. "What more have you found out about my mother? Does she know what happened to Adelis and me? Is she still on Limnos? Has anything worse chanced?"

"And how did you find out about her?" Pen put in.

Tanar glanced at Bosha much the way Nikys had lately glanced at Pen, seeking some permission. So, the two shared their secrets?

Bosha, after a contemplative sip of watered wine, chose to answer Pen: "My elder sister is an acolyte of the Daughter's Order on Limnos. I visit her now and then. She was thus aware of Lady Tanar's interest in General Arisaydia, so when Madame Gardiki was brought in, she sent me a private note."

"I didn't think men were allowed to enter the Order's precincts," said Pen, confused.

Bosha cast him a head-tilt, and said dryly, "That is correct."

Pen gulped back an apology, in a dim notion that it would just make things worse. *Likely so*, murmured Des. He flushed slightly. Bosha seemed more grimly amused than offended at his discomfiture.

Bosha added to Nikys, "Your mother is still at the Order. Unharmed as far as we know. We haven't followed up with further inquiries, because such are dangerous should they fall into the wrong hands."

Penric wondered just whose hands those were, and what weapons they held. He supposed he'd find out in due course. Preferably not the hard way.

Bosha addressed the air between Nikys and Penric: "So what is your plan for freeing her?"

Nikys scrubbed her fingers through her curls, in disarray after the day's travel. "All my mind has been fixed on just getting here. We get out to the island somehow, get her out somehow. Penric thinks we should make the return journey by sea, being already there."

"By choice not on a Cedonian ship," Pen put in. "Adriac, with luck"—Nikys shot him a sharp look—"but it will depend on what we can find most swiftly to hand."

"Will that be the safest course?" said Tanar doubtfully. "I mean...storms. Pirates."

"Storms I can do nothing about," Penric granted. "Pirates are no problem." Once they drew close enough, anyway. Letting a chaos demon loose to do her worst in some other ship's rigging than the one they were on ought to have remarkable results.

Oh, yes, murmured Des, in gleeful anticipation; Pen gathered she'd be disappointed if pirates *didn't* show up.

Nikys nodded untroubled understanding at this last. Tanar and Bosha stared, startled.

After a moment, Bosha went on, "So, you arrive, you leave, and in between, what? A miracle occurs? Your plan seems to be missing its middle."

"I have never been to Thasalon before," said Pen, carefully not saying, *You are its middle.* He suspected Bosha suspected this. "I must rely on Nikys and local knowledge for this part, but I'll do all I can in support of her."

"Penric smuggled Adelis and me out of Cedonia to Orbas the first time," Nikys put in, "and he'd never been there before either. He is not without skills." Of course, not saying what kind rather left this assertion dangling in air.

Tanar nodded, accepting this without question. Bosha as plainly did not.

Tanar rubbed her delicate neck. Her girlish figure could not compete with Nikys's lush build, but her shining hair, braided up on her head in a complex weave with a glimmer of pearls, had reddish highlights in the candle-glow that Pen thought might show auburn in daylight, and her eyes were a clear hazel tending to the gold side. Fine skin, good teeth. It seemed it was not just her fortune that had attracted Adelis to her, and besides, at the time of his late courtship, his wealth had matched hers. Penric had more trouble imagining what had attracted Tanar to Adelis.

Oh, come, Pen, Des scoffed. *Adelis is a very compelling man. Profoundly irritating at moments, I'll give you that, but when not being an ass, and you must allow he's had a great deal to throw him off-balance of late, ladies might find him quite magnetic.*

Even disfigured as he is now? Stripped of his Cedonian properties?

Of course. Really, after eleven years with us, I should think you would understand women better.

Lady Tanar still seemed to care about him, anyway, which was entirely to their benefit.

More interestingly, in two years no other suitor has nipped in and carried her off, Des pointed out. *I can't imagine it's for lack of trying, not with her purse.*

Tanar placed a small, decisive fist upon the table. "It's plain we can do nothing more tonight. I think it's best if you stay right in here with us, Nikys, concealed. You can sleep with me. Sura can find a place for your, um, traveling companion." She eyed Pen more doubtfully, but gestured at them both. "Is this all you came with?"

Pen thought of the duke's coins, sewn in hems or otherwise concealed about both their persons, but said only, "We left our luggage in the outer garden."

"Won't there be servants about?" asked Nikys. "Can they be trusted?"

"Sura will keep them out from underfoot," said Tanar, with an assured nod. "He generally does anyway." She rose, and the rest of them perforce followed.

"Best not to involve them yet," said Bosha. "That being the case, do show me to your belongings, Master Penric."

"Certainly, Master Bosha."

Bosha lit and took up a small glass candle lantern, and guided Pen out into the darkened gallery. His footfalls moved soft across the boards, and Pen tried to match the quiet as he followed the eunuch down the end stairs, through a crooked passage, and to a door in the outer end wall, locked and barred for the night. Pen wondered if Nikys had guided them in this way, might he not have come so close to being knifed? He studied Bosha's pale braid, swinging down his back as they followed through what was no dark to Des, and gave it no better than even odds.

They wound through the garden to the concealing bush. Pen collected his medical case himself, and his other satchel, leaving Bosha to take up Nikys's valise. Bosha lifted it and gazed thoughtfully around.

"How did you gain entry through the outer wall?"

"Nikys knew of the postern door."

"It should have been locked."

"I'm good with locks."

"Is that so."

They'd just started back when the dogs came rushing up again. Still barkless, fortunately, although they managed a growl at Bosha, returned in kind. Enough of the geas lingered that they still fawned around Pen.

"Our dogs are not normally so useless, either," said Bosha, wading through them after his uninvited guest.

"Animals like me. And I think they recognized Nikys," Pen offered.

As the main house loomed before them, Bosha added in a cool tone, "You should not have been able to defeat that lock. Past the lock, you should not have slipped by the dogs. Past the dogs"—he turned his head—"you should not have been able to mount the balcony. On the balcony, you should not have been able to evade my knife. Yet you somehow did all of these things, Master Penric."

"…Madame Khatai did not choose me for her courier for no reason, sir."

"Hnh." Bosha added after a moment, "I quite dislike being troubled to be the last man between the hazards of the world and Lady Tanar. It takes the maids so much effort to scrub the blood out of the floorboards."

Was that a jest? Pen cleared his throat. "It's a rich estate. Are thieves a common problem for you here?"

Bosha shrugged. "Ordinary thieves are a task for the other retainers. Lady Xarre's mandate to me is more exclusive."

"Is her daughter Tanar under some special threat?"

"Say constant, rather. One too-persistent rejected suitor, last year, actually tried a more direct abduction. Why he thought he would gain forgiveness, after, I cannot imagine. Or that his hirelings would keep his secrets. We left the bodies at his front gate to be found in the morning. I believe he took the hint."

Not a jest, then, murmured Des. Pen would rather she didn't sound so pleased.

"I see," said Pen, wondering what hint he was supposed to be taking.

Oh, I think it's quite clear, said Des. ...*You know, I'm beginning to like this fellow. If there are any markers for a child of the Bastard he has missed, I can't picture them. Now I am curious about his birth.*

We're not asking, Des.

Back in the sitting chamber, Bosha knocked on an adjoining door, evidently to the lady's bedchamber. Tanar opened it brightly, received Nikys's case, and bade them both a cheery goodnight. Pen could hear her and Nikys's voices, quietly speaking, as the door swung shut again. Bosha led to a matching door on the opposite inner wall, opening it to another bedchamber.

He lit a brace of candles, and Penric took in a carved writing table, shelves crammed with books and papers, chests and a wardrobe along the walls, a washstand, and a narrow bed piled with folded clothing. Bosha removed the garments perfunctorily to the tops of a couple of the chests, and gestured. "You can have my bed."

"Where will you sleep?"

"Where I usually do." He plucked nightclothes from a hook on the inside of the wardrobe and vanished back to the sitting room, shutting the door behind him.

Nonplussed, but mortally tired, Pen took advantage of the washstand, then changed into his own nightshirt. He poked briefly around the room. Bosha seemed to own a great deal more clothing than an average servant, much more finely made. The books and papers were too many to take in, but seemed mostly of a utilitarian nature—apparently, he really was Tanar's secretary. Among his other more disturbing duties. A number of drawers and chests were locked, which wouldn't have slowed Pen down had he further reason to pry.

Curious, and concerned because while the eunuch had put himself between Pen and Tanar, fair enough, he had also put himself between Pen and *Nikys*, Pen cracked the door to the sitting room and checked. Bosha, wearing a nightshirt of fine lawn, was just unrolling a wool-stuffed linen mattress down before Lady Tanar's door. An unsheathed short sword with a chased blade sat propped by the doorjamb.

Is that one tainted too, Des?

Seems to be. I long to ask him what he is using, and how he compounds it. You ought to find that professionally interesting as well.

Do you think he brews up his own drugs? Those locked chests were suddenly more interesting.

Do you imagine he doesn't?

A faint sound of feminine voices penetrated from the closed door beyond. Pen bet Bosha wasn't above putting his ear to it.

Nor are you, Pen dear, but it seems the position is taken.

Pen was too exhausted to fret further tonight. Judging that they were both about as sincere as two strange cats, he exchanged polite nods with Bosha and withdrew.

VI

WHILE WAITING FOR the men to return
with their baggage, Tanar drew Nikys into
her bedchamber. She sat before her dressing table
and began, a bit awkwardly, to take down her braids
for the night.

"Shall I help you?" asked Nikys, moving behind
her.

"Oh, would you please? Sura usually does it, but
with you here he won't intrude."

"My pleasure." Nikys began to withdraw the
pearl pins and drop them into the enameled bowl
that Tanar shifted closer.

To watch Nikys, Tanar angled the glass mirror in
its wooden arms, and sat straight. "It's so good to see

you well, though I'm sorry it took such a terrifying errand to bring you to me again. Adelis was the only one of my suitors with the wit to offer me a *sister.*"

Nikys smiled, flattered. In their early acquaintance Tanar had looked up to her—ten years older and once married—as a fount of female wisdom on how men and women dealt with each other in the bedchamber. Nikys had eventually determined that this was not because Tanar had been left untutored, but rather that she was collecting intelligence from as many sources as possible. Preparing for her life's journey, like Penric studying Duke Jurgo's maps before they'd left Vilnoc. That Nikys had elected to be frank and clear, just as she would have wished for herself, had been much valued.

"Adelis…" Tanar began again more tentatively. "Do you know how he still feels about me? I wrote him a few times while he was on campaign, but received no reply."

"That's just Adelis," Nikys reassured her, beginning to unwind auburn braids. "He doesn't reply to me either when he's in the field, but I know he saves my letters." Now lost with the rest of their possessions. "He was hurried off to Patos so swiftly after the Rusylli campaign, with no triumphal celebration even offered in the capital. And then he had to master his new command. I think he was already starting to be wary. If he suspected trouble was coming down on him, he wouldn't have wanted to involve you."

Tanar's face set in a grave grimace. "I'm very afraid I might have been involved despite myself. Did you know Minister Methani's nephew, Lord Bordane, has been one of my more persistent suitors?"

Adelis had suspected that Methani's cabal, close around the emperor at court, had engineered his downfall by the subtle half-forged correspondence with the Duke of Adria. That was to say, Adelis's letter to Adria had been forged; the return reply had been condemningly real, and guided forthwith into his enemies' outstretched hands.

"It's a hideous thought," continued Tanar, "but as soon as I had heard what had happened to Adelis in Patos, I wondered how much might have been a ploy to get him permanently out of Lord Bordane's way." She raised quietly stricken eyes to Nikys's, in the mirror.

Nikys considered this, watching the guilty fear fleeting in Tanar's face. "That might have been a factor," she said hesitantly, "but it certainly wasn't that alone. Adelis and Methani had been clashing at court for years before this. Adelis's recent success against the Rusylli, and so his rising popularity with his troops, are far more likely to have set this off. I can't speak for Lord Bordane, but I guarantee Methani's more worried about threats to the emperor from a potential usurper than about his nephew's love-life." Imagined threats, curse him— all of this horror done for fears made of vapor and slander. "The latter might simply have been a bonus, from their point of view." Granted Methani would not be immune to the appeal of bringing Tanar's wealth into his clan.

Tanar took this in, and slowly nodded. More relieved by this honesty than by some airy denial, and no wonder Nikys liked her. Had Adelis appreciated her character, as well as her lively beauty?

"Is Lord Bordane still persistent?" Nikys took up the hairbrush from the table and began untangling Tanar's tresses.

Tanar made a moue. "Among others. Up until my last birthday Mother held them all off for me, playing the rigid guardian, but now I'm at my legal majority, they know I could consent on my own. They try all kinds of tricks to get me alone to hear their pleas. Sura is most annoyed." Her puff of disdain transmuted to a purr of pleasure as Nikys changed to longer, more soothing strokes. "Oh, that's almost as good as Sura."

That a eunuch servant acted sometimes as a lady's maid was no very unusual thing. Tanar's morning habit of brushing and braiding Bosha's white hair in turn had been more startling, when Nikys had glimpsed it on her last overnight visit. It was evidently a custom lingering from when Tanar had been a tyrannical six-year-old princess of the house, treating her new guardian, to his bemusement, as something between a playmate, a large doll, and a compliant slave. Most other innocent intimacies from that era had fallen away with Tanar's more conscious maturity, to Bosha's silent regret, Nikys gathered.

"Do none of your other suitors tempt you?"

Tanar shrugged. "I confess, your brother was the first man to really do so."

"It's become rather hopeless," Nikys observed, reluctantly conscientious. "It will be long before he can rebuild his fortune, if ever. You are anchored to Cedonia by your own possessions, and he cannot cross the border."

"Politics change." Her soft mouth set mulishly. "I can afford to wait."

"Do you want him to wait? Should I tell him so?" Nikys hesitated, though her hands kept moving. "Do you love him that much?"

Tanar, after a moment, returned candor for candor. "I'm not sure. Setting all the pretty poetry aside as beguiling blither, because I've never met anyone who seems to actually think like that, I don't know what love is supposed to be. I care that he should be well. The thought of him being injured or killed distresses me. When we had the news of his blinding"—a shudder passed through her—"I cried and carried on till poor Sura was quite alarmed. Of *course* I knew enough to compose myself before I left our chambers." She tossed her head in some remembered irritation.

After a few more strokes, she added in a lower voice, "I thought for a while, before Patos, that I might use *waiting for Adelis* as a stick to fend off the others, but not if it could call down more danger on his head. Because assassins can cross borders where armies cannot."

Nikys sighed, unable to gainsay this, but pointed out, "Given the hazards of his profession, I think that should be one of your lesser worries." And, more thoughtfully: "It might be better for a soldier's wife not to love too much."

Tanar's gaze sought hers in the mirror, just obliquely enough to ask: "Do you still miss your husband Kymis?"

Nikys drew a cool breath through her nostrils. So many memories, and the good ones, in a strange way, almost more painful than the bad, so that she preferred to put them all away in the same locked box. "Not so much now. The present drives out the past, a little more each day."

A knock sounded at the chamber door, and Tanar went to receive Nikys's valise from the hands of her servant, whom she bade a fond goodnight. Both women broke off to share out the washstand and don nightgowns. Tanar's spacious bed seemed the most inviting road-weary Nikys had ever seen, and she fell into it gratefully as Tanar blew out the candles.

In the darkness, Tanar remarked, "Your courier fellow, Penric—Daughter's blessings, what a fetching young man. I've not seen that color of hair or eyes except among the emperor's southern-island guard, and nothing like so bright."

"Not so young," said Nikys. "He's thirty." *And it's the Bastard's blessings. Theologically speaking. Maybe that explains it all...*

"Really? The same age as you?" Tanar seemed to mull this. In a tone of sly humor, she murmured, "Do you fancy him?"

Nikys made a neutral noise.

"Because you're a widow, as free as a woman can be. I don't suppose there's any insurmountable barrier of rank between you." An envious sigh. "And he looked as if he liked you. I quite think you could have him, if you wanted him," she rippled on in cheerful, grating speculation. "Do you know very much about his background?"

"I'm beginning to."

Tanar nudged her with her elbow. "Do tell?"

"Not my tale." Starting with, *He's the agent who carried the fatal letter from the duke of Adria,* descending through *He's a Temple sorcerer with ten other women's ghosts living inside his head,* and going on to *He could knock a dozen soldiers to the ground with a twitch of his eyebrow,* and Master Bosha *really* wouldn't like that news. Not to mention being a physician of near-miraculous powers too broken to practice his craft, a scholar in half-a-dozen languages with enough reputation to be coveted by the duke of Orbas, and a man so very, very far away from home. "It's complicated."

Tanar made a noise of disappointment, but pressed no further.

After a little, Tanar added, "I was so sorry I hadn't had a chance to meet Madame Gardiki. Adelis spoke of inviting your mother to Thasalon for the purpose, but then the Rusylli interrupted. And all the rest followed."

"Well. I can't say he's ever mentioned wanting to do so for any other woman. I think she would like you."

A hopeful sort of "Mm?"

"Do you really think we will be able to get her out?" All the worrisome unknowns still ahead of them made Nikys's head throb to contemplate. Bosha had placed his elegant thumb square upon the problem. *And then a miracle occurs.*

No. As they gained more information, they would find a route through. Somehow. Step by step. She couldn't work miracles, but she knew she could work *work*.

Tanar, Nikys thought, also hesitated between kindness and candor. Nikys could not tell which side Tanar imagined she was coming down on when she at last stated confidently, "Sura will know how."

Nikys let that sit unchallenged. She had put hope before prudence, or why else had she come this far? A few more breaths, in the dark. Hope or prayer, she offered up: "I always wanted to have a sister, too."

"Let us try to make that happen, then," said Tanar softly.

VII

$\mathcal{P}$EN WOKE TO early morning light filtering through the shutters, and low voices from the sitting room. He snapped awake and went to check through the adjoining door, to see Bosha, barefoot and wearing his trousers but no shirt, turning away from the gallery door having received a large tray from some servant, which he set on the round table.

Bosha also sported a long, old scar running diagonally across his back, crooked from some crude sewing-up. Like the one on his lip? Pen didn't even need to say *Sight, Des,* to be given a deeper view. Sword cut, surely. As Bosha turned, raising his face sharply to Pen, Pen also marked a set of scars of the same age on his arms. *Defensive wounds, would you say, Des?*

Oh, aye.

Even inured by his anatomical training, it seemed rude to Pen to glance below the man's waistband, but Des had no such inhibitions. The significant scar there seemed older, surgical and clean. No signs, as Pen had for an instant feared, of being relict of some brutal battlefield mutilation, as sometimes happened. Bosha was otherwise intact, not always the case either, the more ruthless and complete cuttings leading to incontinence and those ugly jokes about stinking court eunuchs. Of which Des, partly through Mira but largely through Vasia, one of Des's old Cedonian riders, knew many, and *I don't want to hear them, Des.*

Suit yourself, Des sniffed. *But all that we know, you'll know in the end.*

Not while I have to look the man in the face. He added no softening courtesies to that one, and trusted Des took the hint.

Bosha, unaware of this uncanny inspection, gave Pen a nod by way of greeting, which Pen returned. He pulled on a long-sleeved linen shirt, gathered at the wrists into ruffles, and added as his somewhat bed-rumpled head emerged, "Let the ladies know the tea is here. I'll be back shortly. Don't answer the door." He padded out barefoot, face tight with thought.

Pen went back to Bosha's bedchamber-that-wasn't and quickly dressed himself, before going to tap on the sitting room's opposite door. Tanar poked her head out, received the news about the tea with sunny pleasure, and went back in. Light feminine voices and mysterious rattling-about preceded, eventually, the emergence of the women. Nikys, Pen noted, looked very fine first thing in the morning. And less tense and tired today than on most of the other mornings of their journey, good.

Nikys wore her day garb, Tanar a pink con-coction that Pen, or rather, Des, decoded as a dressing-gown, not some fanciful court wear. Only two teacups had arrived with the pot and covered plates and basket, and Pen adroitly evaded sitting lest Lady Tanar feel compelled to try to give up her cup to her other guest.

The social dilemma was solved in a few minutes when Bosha returned with spare cups hooked on the fingers of one hand and a larger pot in the other. Three cups, not two, Pen noted as they were dealt out. The plates and basket proved to contain new-baked rolls, slices of soft white cheese, boiled eggs, olives, and fresh grapes, in sufficient abundance to share around without constraint. Also some of those ghastly dried fish blocks, which Pen avoided and everyone else seemed to think were food. Practical munching replaced conversation for a little.

Bosha rose immediately at a firm rap on the chamber door, seeming unsurprised, though Tanar jerked around in alarm. He opened the door only wide enough to admit the visitor, favoring her with that hand-over-the-heart bow—Pen could not decide if the gesture was ironic or sincere—and closed it with a click in her wake. Nikys and Tanar stood up respectfully, and Pen copied them.

Lady Xarre, without doubt. Tanar, Nikys had told Pen, was the child of the lady's later age much as Adelis had been for Lady Florina. It had been a second marriage for both her and Lord Xarre, who had died when Tanar was four or five. Something of a love match, Nikys had implied. No mention of non-surviving older siblings.

Pen's first impression of *elderly* was not quite correct, he judged. Lady Xarre was a finely dressed, slightly built older woman, to be sure, her graying hair wound up in jewel-pinned braids. The carved wooden cane upon which she leaned was not an affectation, but a needed prop, for Bosha took her other arm and supported her to his chair with no demur on her part.

Des's quick glance by Sight reported, *Very bad hip joints.* Back when he was training and practicing in Martensbridge, Pen had enjoyed some luck persuading such deteriorations to rebuild themselves from within by repeated small applications of uphill magic over weeks or months. Which wasn't time he was going to have, here, so there was no point thinking about it, right? He arranged his lips into a wary smile as she settled herself and looked up at him, and across at Nikys who, following Tanar, had sat again.

"My lady," murmured Bosha. "Madame Khatai you know; may I present to you Master Penric, her courier."

"Lady Xarre," Pen managed.

"Master Penric." At Lady Xarre's wave Pen, too, ducked a bow and reseated himself.

Bosha poured tea for his senior mistress and took a pose leaning against the wall with his arms folded. Pen had seen servants who could fade into the furniture doing that; Bosha really wasn't one of them.

"Surakos told me we had unexpected visitors," Lady Xarre began mildly.

Nikys lifted her chin. "Uninvited, I am afraid. You have my apologies, but under the circumstances I cannot offer regrets."

"Not entirely uninvited. It appears." She cast a pointed glance at Tanar, who squirmed, thus answering the question of whether that note to Nikys had been authorized by Lady Xarre or not. "But not unwelcome, I promise you." Hard to tell how sincere that was. "Given the circumstances. But we are truly in want of first-hand news of the events in Patos, and after." No mistaking the sincerity of that. "You know court rumors. What are not lies outright are invariably so muddled as to be almost worse."

Nikys nodded. She took a deep breath, and launched into a clipped description of the disaster in Patos starting from Adelis's arrest through to his return to Nikys's house, blinded and scalded. She left out the screaming and begging-for-death parts. Pen thought Lady Xarre and Bosha could fill in the lacunae.

"And where do you come into this tale, Master Penric?" Lady Xarre inquired of him.

Nikys bit her lip, caught between her promises to Pen and her unwillingness to lie to her hostess. Pen took up the banner: "Madame Khatai hired me on as a sort of male attendant to her injured brother. I was able to assist her in the sickroom, and later, when General Arisaydia's sight came back, on their flight to Orbas." Which wasn't even untrue.

"That must have been a difficult journey," said Lady Xarre.

"Yes," said Nikys. Pen was a little disappointed that she did not add, *We wouldn't have made it without Penric,* but he had after all asked her not to draw undue attention to him. No one to blame but himself.

Lady Xarre accepted this uninviting monosyllable with a purse of her lips, and did not press for details. She turned to Pen instead. "So much for Orbas. But why were you willing to come here to Thasalon, Master Penric?"

Pen thought over the impossible chaos his life had become ever since he'd first set foot in Cedonia, and decided to try a shorter truth. "I'm courting Madame Khatai."

Pen wished Nikys looked half so delighted with this statement as Tanar did. Lady Xarre smiled dryly.

Pen couldn't tell if Bosha's expression was a smirk or just his lip scar.

"Have you known each other long, then?" asked Lady Xarre.

Nikys answered, "No. We just met in Patos."

Her voice still as pleasantly level, Lady Xarre said, "Do you trust him?"

Nikys's eyes squeezed closed, opened. "With my life, yes," she said, with gratifying firmness. "With my future...I'm still thinking."

Lady Xarre chuckled. "Wise girl." She drained her cup—Bosha bent to refill it—and leaned back in her chair. "I confess," she said, "I, too, would be happy to see Madame Gardiki safe with her son and daughter in Orbas. Could she somehow be magically transported there."

Pen flinched. Nikys coughed, and drank tea.

"Surakos reports you seemed a trifle unclear about the intervening steps."

Pen suspected Surakos had been a lot more blunt than that. "We actually hope to borrow his knowledge, as neither Madame Khatai nor I have even been to Limnos, and he has. Everything has to start with understanding both the physical layout and the human defenses. The Order's house cannot be as impenetrable as a prison or a fortress, if it hosts visitors and pilgrims. Not to mention the need for transporting food and supplies in and out for its inhabitants—how many?"

Lady Xarre waved at Bosha, who dutifully replied, "About three hundred Temple-sworn divines, acolytes, and dedicats, and perhaps an equal number of lay dedicats in service to them. All women, within the precincts. The complex of buildings sits on a notable promontory. Beyond the single drawbridge there is a rambling villa for male dedicats of the goddess, and guards. No men ever set foot past the bridge."

That was more populated than Pen had been picturing. "Do men ever try? People being what they are. In disguise, perhaps."

Bosha really smirked, this time. "People being what they are, the Order has a cadre of sacred dogs that roam the entry courtyard, trained to sniff out males. All bitches."

In both senses, Pen gathered. "That actually works?"

"Extremely well, I'm told."

Tanar looked up. "Do you confuse them, Sura dear?"

"I admit, I once made some amusing experiments borrowing your perfume, but in any case I am known, there."

"Did the perfume work?" Pen asked, intent.

"I couldn't really tell." Rose-colored eyes glanced from under lowered lids. "I suspect it would not work for you."

But I have other ways of controlling dogs. "Do you know, or have you a guess, where and how Madame Gardiki may be kept within the walls?"

Bosha shrugged. "She may have the freedom of the precincts, and mix with the residents. Some long-term lady prisoners have in the past, if they were judged docile enough. More likely, being new and untried, she would be kept in a locked chamber. Possibly on the side overlooking the sea. The Order is mainly guarded by its, ah, geology. And the water, wind, and currents. The island is only five miles long."

At Pen's prodding, Bosha went on to describe more details of the architecture and the residents' daily rounds of work and prayer. He seemed a remarkably observant man. Pen was getting less and less surprised at this.

"And how do the prelates of the Daughter's Order feel about their goddess's house being used as an imperial prison?"

Bosha cocked his head. "Interesting question. But since the imperial court is one of the main financial supports of the retreat, I don't suppose they can refuse the duty."

"The visitors who go in and out—are they counted?"

"Yes. There is a visitor's book, which gets marked off. And rechecked at sunset, when the drawbridge is raised for the night. The ladies do value their privacy."

Pen sat back and rubbed his knuckles across his lips. *Des, do you see any possibilities?*

Do you even remember who you are talking to, lad? and that was, without question, Learned Ruchia's voice that scoffed at him. *I can see six offhand, but let's start with the quietest. The one that involves setting the place afire being the very last resort.*

I should think so! Pen shuddered at this hypothetical offense to the Lady of Spring.

Let me ask Nikys a few questions.

Pen yielded control of his mouth to his demon, and turned. "Nikys, what does your mother look like? Is she tall, short, fat, thin? Skin color, eyes and hair?"

"She's a little taller than I am, and, um, not so round. Her coloring is much like mine."

"Is she very level-headed in emergencies?"

"Well, she raised Adelis and me." Nikys's enchanting grin, too seldom seen of late, flickered. "Following my father around to various army camps, to boot. I'm too young to remember the one time we were all in the baggage train when it was attacked, though I've heard the stories. Drema was always the practical one, of our two mothers. Florma was the nervous one." Their children's old nicknames for Idrene and Lady Florina. "I think my mother would have liked to be more nervous, at times, but the role was taken. So she mostly ended up reassuring us and Florma all together."

"I see." He glanced at Lady Xarre's cane, propped against her chair. "How fit is she, physically? Can she walk, run, climb, ride?"

"Fit enough. She's only just fifty now. She can do all those things, though not like a young man, of course." She mulled. "Maybe not what you mean by climb. Not even when she was young. Me either. Stairs we can manage."

Des hummed aloud. "I think a substitution removal might just work, here."

"Beg pardon?" said Nikys.

"Two pilgrims enter the precincts to make prayer. A woman and her niece. Mm, cousin. Friend, anyway.

We find Madame Gardiki and exchange clothes, and other things as needed. Later, two women sign out again, and make their way to their boat. Except the woman left in the cell is not Madame Gardiki. I escape at my leisure, and rejoin you." Pen wasn't sure whose voice was speaking, now.

"What?" said Nikys. "You don't look anything like my mother!"

"It's not as if we could leave you. That would be like trading a gold coin for a gold coin."

Tanar said tentatively, "Might I do?"

Lady Xarre and Bosha both replied, instantly and in unison, "No!"

Tanar ducked her chin, peeved. "I would like to do something. I could be the only person here with the right to drink from the goddess's well, after all."

"No," Bosha repeated. "There must be nothing whatsoever to connect this escapade with the Xarre household. Or with my sister Hekat at the Order, for that matter. She's the only member of my family I could ever stand, and vice versa. I am wholly loth to risk her." He frowned back at Tanar, and at Pen. "And if you are imagining involving me any further in this, may I point out that I am a line leading straight back to both."

"Yes, you are much too physically memorable," agreed Pen. Although evidently an adept and ruthless bodyguard, which was an undoubted value.

"So are you," Nikys pointed out.

"Appearances can be changed. In both directions. Sometimes by quite simple means. My hair and skin could be colored, or we might obtain a blond wig. I have Mira's clogs in my luggage, which could boost your mother's height to mimic mine. Eyes, well, who notices eyes?"

"Yours?" said Nikys. "Everybody."

Pen was a little miffed when all in the room nodded solemn agreement.

But Bosha pushed off from his wall. "I might have a solution for that." He trod off to his bedchamber, and returned with a small case in his hand. He opened it to display a pair of spectacles in fine brass frames, but the lenses were dark green glass.

"Oh!" said Pen, bending to peer closely. "That's very clever! I know a lens-grinder in Martensbridge who would like to know about that. Not that the sun is a great hazard in the cantons, although sometimes the sun on the snow is blinding."

"You have sun and snow at the same time?" said Nikys in some wonder. "What a strange country you come from, Pen."

Pen noted that slip of the tongue, *Pen*, and cut off a smile.

"They were a gift from Lady Xarre," said Bosha. "When I first became a retainer of the household. Because my eyes watered and hurt in the noonday light. In twenty-six years before that, no one had ever thought of offering me such an aid. I've no desire to give them to you, but if it will get you out of here faster, I will."

"They can be replaced, Surakos dear," murmured Lady Xarre.

A hand-on-heart silent nod of thanks. Ah, no, that wasn't irony, was it.

Pen picked them up with care and tried them on. The lenses were flat, thankfully, without any headache-inducing distortions. He blinked around at his viridescent audience.

"If you want unmemorable," said Nikys, "that's not it either."

"So much the better. People will remember the spectacles but not the face behind them."

"Maybe... So would you be Mira again?"

The other three people in the room stared at him curiously, and Bastard's tears—or belly-laugh, whichever—that wasn't a story he wanted told here.

Or anywhere. "Not Mira, gods forfend, not at the Daughter's Order. Learned Ruchia. She'll know what to do, for one thing."

Nikys nodded, satisfied. Everyone else kept staring.

"Dyes," said Tanar after a moment. "Now that *is* something I might help with!"

VIII

NIKYS HAD BEEN in Tanar's stillroom before. Penric had not, and looked surprised when he was shown past Bosha's bedchamber through the next door down to find the workbench, the shelves crammed with neatly labeled jars and notebooks, the chests with dozens of tiny drawers, and the neat array of tools. The room even featured a little stove with a vent to the outside. Tanar opened the shutters to let in the light; only a window, here, no balcony.

"This is as well-stocked as any apothecary shop," said Penric, gazing around. Nikys expected he was qualified to judge.

"Yes," said Tanar cheerfully. "I first became interested in the art when I made Sura teach me how he concocted his, hm, medicines. Then I followed Karaji around and had her show me how she made all the dyes for the household's spinning and weaving. Then Mama permitted me a real apothecary as a tutor—she came out once a week for, oh, almost three years. So I can make all the household's remedies. I'm better at it than Sura, now."

The retainer gifted her with a conceding eyebrow-lift—proud teacher?—and she tossed her head in pleased reply.

Penric's smile had grown oddly fixed. "Can you cook, too?"

"Oh, yes. Mother agrees I should learn every skill I can. Because even when supervising servants, one needs to understand their tasks. And who knows what all an officer's wife might be called upon to do?"

"A general's wife," stated Bosha, as if repeating himself from some prior and fruitless protest, "would surely have proper help."

Nikys laughed. "So people imagine. I think Tanar has a better grip on the possibilities."

"Mother made it a bargain," explained Tanar. "She would trade me a tutor in whatever I fancied in exchange for me studying her bookkeeping, which I do not love. It all worked out. Except for the horse-shoeing, that time."

"Horseshoeing?" said Nikys. Even she hadn't heard this tale. Bosha, who evidently had, hid his mouth behind his hand.

"We had a very patient old pony, and a very patient old farrier. Who both grew much less patient as the day wore on. I still don't think I could shoe a horse, but if ever my horse threw a shoe, I wager I could nail it back on without laming the poor beast, so there's that much." She looked around. "But I like the stillroom best."

Nikys directed Pen to light the stove. The two women donned aprons and set about mixing up an array of samples. They then made him sit on a stool and remove his shirt, testing the colors on his skin until they achieved a tolerable match for Nikys. While Tanar expanded the recipe, Nikys, who had done the task before, combed an inky black dye through Penric's unbound hair.

"Such a shame," Tanar murmured over her shoulder, watching this eclipse.

"My hair has been recolored so many times since I came to Cedonia I'm surprised it hasn't all fallen out," sighed Penric. "I'm tempted to shave my head to defend myself."

"Don't you dare," said Nikys, giving a lock a sharp tug, forgetting that she wasn't supposed to care. Pen, the rat, noticed, because he pressed down a smile.

"With the fixative I'm using these dyes should stand up to water and washing for a few days," said Tanar. "Be careful not to let them rub off on anything where someone might notice."

Once the skin treatment was satisfactorily started, Tanar and Bosha vanished out the gallery door together. Nikys, trying not to think too much about this excuse for so pleasurably touching him, ended up coloring Pen's face, neck, hands, arms and shoulders, then started at his feet, working up his long legs to his knees.

Pen swallowed. She braced herself for who-knew-what—whatever had possessed him to tell the world he was courting her?—but he said, unexpectedly, "Did you know Bosha carries poisoned blades?"

"I knew he went armed. I mean, he needs to. I didn't know about the other." Although it made sense to Nikys. The eunuch was not a man who could expect mercy if he lost a fight, and Tanar was not a charge he dared fail.

"Do you think Tanar brews his poisons?"

Nikys tilted her head, considering this. "Very possibly. She'd love to think she was doing something for him, in exchange for all he does for her."

"That doesn't bother you?"

"It seems a very good skill for a woman who, by marriage or some other ill-chance, could well be tossed into the imperial court at Thasalon. Which is the most poisonous place I've ever been, even without the aid of apothecaries."

"Could be hard on an unsatisfactory husband. Doesn't it make you worry for Adelis?"

Nikys's lips twitched. "Not really. Adelis is not the sort of man who inspires poisoning. He's the sort of man who inspires hitting on the head with a skillet."

Penric muffled a too-agreeing snort. "So speaks his loving sister. Have you ever done so?"

"Not since we were twelve, I admit." She added after a moment, "Then he grew too tall to reach. Bad angle for the swing."

"I'll keep that in mind."

"You're safe. You're even taller."

A snicker. But then, annoyingly, he rose, leaving her with dye dripping through her fingers, and began tapping his way around the cabinets. A pause, a familiar click, and he drew one door wide and stuck his head in.

"Hey! I imagine that was locked for a reason!"

"Oh," he breathed, "indeed it was." He sounded a little too delighted. "What do you make of it all, Des?...Really?...Huh."

"Stop snooping," she said, undercutting her indignation by adding, "Someone might come back."

After a long look he closed it up again, to her relief, and troubled to relock it, too.

"You can't go about piebald. Come back here."

Dutifully, he returned, sat, and gave her back his leg. "Interesting."

And left it at that, till she gave in and growled, "All right, what? You're obviously itching to tell."

"Fast-acting paralytics, mostly, according to Des. The death is in the dose, as they say. Even packed in a grooved blade, I don't think such low amounts would kill. *Clever* bastard."

Nikys reflected. "Right. All Bosha'd have to do is land one nick to slow his opponent down. Then kill him with his steel, if he had to. No question of poisoning would ever arise, after. And if someone got his blade away from him, they couldn't kill him with it. Not with the venom, at least."

Penric, who had opened his mouth, said plaintively, "I was going to explain that."

"No need. Have you ever listened to a crowd of drunken army louts bragging about their exploits to each other? One learns a lot." Not that the men noticed.

"Since escaping my brother Drovo-the-aspiring-mercenary at a fairly early age, I've mostly managed to avoid such experiences."

"Lucky you."

Pen was sitting drying, and Nikys was fanning him to speed the process, when Tanar and Bosha came back with piles of clothing in their arms. They proved to be borrowings from some senior female servants, sober and sedate. The key factor in selection, once Nikys and Tanar bound Pen's dye-damp hair in a cloth and marshaled him through a try-on, turned out to be length, but he only needed the one change. Pen seemed much more adept out-fitting the persona he'd dubbed *Learned Ruchia* than the first time, when trying to dress, and perhaps evoke, the courtesan Mira. Was he a fast learner—well, Nikys knew he was—or was Ruchia simply closer to himself? Or were all his internal ladies equally present to him?

Partway into this process, Bosha, who had kept his amusement almost under control, though Pen had certainly noticed the voiceless sniggers, inclined his head in a shadow-bow and withdrew through the gallery door. After some fussing about and much debate, they finished the transformation. Pen took a turn around the small stillroom practicing the management of his draperies and a very convincing feminine walk.

"I really do believe you will be able to slip into the Order's precincts," said Tanar, admiring her handiwork. "But will you be able to get out again safely? By yourself?"

Bosha reentered through his own chamber door in time to hear this, and leaned against the jamb. "I expect so. As Madame Khatai says, he has skills." Nikys looked up to see him twirling Pen's Temple braids around one long index finger. "And now we know what kind."

Pen went rigid, and so, for a moment, did Nikys, chilled with a sudden realization of how very, very *dangerous* an act it might be to bait Pen. But Pen only licked his lips and said, flatly, "Give those back."

"Certainly." Bosha handed them across at arm's length. Two arms' lengths, counting Pen's side.

Tanar, goggling, said, "Are those sorcerer's braids?"

"Yes," said Pen shortly.

"Are they real?" A reasonable question, given all the exercises in disguise.

"Yes."

"That explains a lot," murmured Bosha, folding his arms, and himself back to the doorjamb.

"Oh my goodness!" said Tanar. "I've never met a sorcerer to talk to. Nikys, did you know? Yes, of course you do." Tanar looked thrilled. Bosha did not.

"Do you normally rifle through your guests' luggage?" said Pen testily.

"Do you normally light a fire without using a taper or spill?" Bosha inquired in turn.

"...Oh."

"Yes, he does," said Nikys. And when had she, and Pen, become so used to this simple domestic convenience that she asked, and he complied, routinely? "Oh, Pen, I'm sorry. I didn't think."

"It's all right," he said, though his voice was still a little choked. "Neither did I. Though I didn't realize he was watching."

"It answers so many questions," said Bosha, "and yet raises so many more. Given where I found them in your case. Temple physician, as well?"

"Not...exactly."

"In all but final oath," Nikys put in on Pen's behalf.

"Because the cadre of physicians, I am given to understand, are the very most adept of Temple sorcerers."

"You understand correctly," said Pen. His mouth reset in a thin line, and only Nikys knew how deep a scar that was for him. Bosha would blunder around and never know why the conversation had turned so sour. That wasn't even touching on the disaster that could ensue should Bosha learn Pen had come to Patos as an agent of the duke of Adria. And still might be one.

She cut in ruthlessly. "Your many questions may be answered in full—should we meet again for Tanar and Adelis's wedding. Here, now, it's better not to know."

Nikys wondered what it said for Bosha's mind that, with a slow nod, he accepted this.

NIKYS SAID farewell to Tanar in her bedchamber. They exchanged fierce hugs.

"Take care," said Tanar, releasing her. "I'm happier now I know more about your courier. A Temple sorcerer, really? *And* a physician?"

"He healed Adelis's eyes," Nikys confirmed. "It wasn't a matter of the executioner doing a poor job. I swear they were half boiled-away."

Tanar gasped.

"It was awful beyond belief. I saw. Pen practically rebuilt them, with his sorcery." She felt strangely glad she was able to finally tell someone. Justice? Bragging? She hardly knew.

"But Adelis's eyes are all right now?"

"He sees perfectly. He just looks different."

Tanar nodded, accepting this with a practical air. "And your fetching physician—has he asked you to marry him yet?"

Nikys thought back to that exhausted, difficult conversation she and Pen had scraped through upon arriving safely in Orbas. "I suppose so."

"You *suppose*? How can you not know?"

"Well, I do know. Yes."

"What, and you didn't seize him with both hands? Sorcerer, physician, that astonishing sunburst of hair? So tall. And those *eyes*. Is it true sorcerers can do amazing things in bed?"

"I...don't know. Probably." And did *not* say, *General Chadro certainly seemed to think so.*

"I'd think you'd at least be more curious." Tanar huffed a disappointed sigh.

"As you are?" Nikys muffled a laugh, and Tanar smiled sheepishly. Nikys went on, "But it's never just Penric. He comes as a set. His chaos demon isn't only a power, she's a person. He's even named her. Desdemona."

Tanar pressed her fingers to her lips, stifling a giggle. "Clever!"

"But there are two people living in his head, not just one. All the time." Well, twelve...thirteen, but there was no way now to go into the full roster. "She's been riding along with him in secret all this visit, your third guest."

Tanar's head tilted. "But not secret to you."

"...No."

"And, clearly, not dangerous enough to warn us." Tanar raised her face, and her eyebrows, in something not quite a question.

"That's a point," Nikys conceded, in not quite an answer. "But I wouldn't just be marrying him. I'd be marrying *her*. The chaos demon. Do you see?"

"I...oh." If this did not take Tanar aback, it at least slowed her down. "Well, you are a careful woman, and the gods attest you have suffered much. I suppose you know your own mind." Her tone hooked a lingering doubt onto the end of this statement.

Nikys shrugged rueful agreement with the unspoken codicil. Who could foresee regrets? Her marriage to Kymis had seemed fine, had *been* fine, until its ghastly truncation. To give one's heart to any living being, even a simple cat, was to risk such loss. Which brought her around once again: "So what would you have me tell Adelis?"

Tanar bit her lip and looked down. "Tell him..." She looked up to meet Nikys's eyes. "Tell him I will wait."

"Are you so sure? It could be a long time. Or never. I've seldom met a young woman who wasn't wild to escape her mother's household and become mistress of her own."

"No matter what she had to marry to do so?" Tanar inquired, amused. "That road is not for me. Daughter and Mother be thanked. My mother and I don't exactly have to live atop each other, here. And she indulges all my interests. Or at least, she praises my successes, and says nothing of all my false starts. Which have been many and sometimes embarrassing, but she claims it's all learning."

Nikys captured and gripped her waving hands. "I'll pass your message along, then, when I get the chance."

Nikys picked up her repacked valise and followed Tanar out to the sitting room, where Penric, all fitted out as Ruchia, and Bosha awaited. To curtail the number of Xarre servants to see them, it had been decided that Bosha himself would drive them to the village on the coast where they could take ship to Limnos, and play male escort to the two lady pilgrims. Nikys trusted that Penric's god— and hers, and possibly Bosha's as well, she'd never asked—appreciated the ironies in that, and would protect them along their way in exchange for, if nothing else, the amusement. When they took the channel boat in the morning, Bosha would travel not with their party, but merely at the same time, as discreetly as he'd ever guarded Tanar.

Bosha had traded his more flamboyant robes for a trim sleeveless tunic and matching trousers in dark dyes, with a long-sleeved linen shirt despite the heat. The somber servant's garb somehow managed to make him an even more striking figure. Tanar evidently thought so, too, for she picked an imaginary speck of lint off his tunic and said, "You look very fine."

He placed his hands on her shoulders in turn. "Take care while I'm gone. Sleep in Lady Xarre's chambers. Obey her."

"I always do."

"No, you don't."

"I will this time. Just for you, Mother Hen." She tapped his nose. "You take care of yourself as well. Don't drag back all bloody again. And I absolutely forbid you to get yourself killed. That's an order!"

That hand-to-heart bow was all the answer he gave. As Tanar turned away, his habitual smirk slipped into a smile of such surpassing tenderness that Nikys's breath caught.

It was gone in a moment, the sardonic mask back in place. She might have thought she'd imagined it, except that she doubted she could ever forget it.

Oh.

I think I need to think about this.

It was then time to be smuggled back through the garden to the postern gate, and on out to the side street.

"Wait here," Bosha instructed them. "I'll bring the cart around." He locked the gate after them with a firm clack.

Penric set down his case and satchel, passed the fold of his dress's draperies over his coiled black hair, and leaned against the garden wall. Nikys did the same. At length, she rested her head back upon the day-warmed stone and sighed, "That may be the most forlorn hope I have ever witnessed."

"Hm?" said Pen.

"Bosha and Tanar. He is in love with her, I believe. And he knows it."

Pen's grunt was neither surprised nor disagreeing. "A high-born heiress and a cut servant twice her age? Forlorn indeed. Surely he knows that, too."

"Oh, yes." Nikys went on thoughtfully, "I'm not so sure she knows she's in love with him."

In a distant tone, Pen remarked, "A person might observe that every other name out of her mouth was not 'Adelis'. Is this a cause for concern?"

"Mm, of a sort. I'll have to think of some non-misleading way of letting my brother know they come as a pair or not at all." She added after a moment, "Rather like you and Des."

A convulsive snort. "Bosha and Tanar are nothing at all like me and Des!"

She cocked an eyebrow up at his indignation. "And what does Des have to say to that?"

A little silence. "Des says you're a very shrewd girl and she likes you." A short pause. "And if I would just get my eyes off your, Des, that's rude! I am not that shallow. Yes, he is." Pen clamped his teeth.

Nikys let that one go by, though the corners of her mouth inched up.

He cleared his throat, and resumed, "I think it would be unwise to make assumptions. Bosha seemed very loyal to Lady Xarre, as well. You might note he went to her without telling Tanar, this morning."

"As was his clear duty and, as it turned out, astute. Good for all of us. Was that a point?"

"More of a line. But it's best not to meddle with things half understood," said Pen. Nikys wasn't sure whether it was Pen or Des who then added, "Or else I would recommend they run off somewhere far away and set up an apothecary shop. They could just live over it, together."

"In a set of rooms?"

"Mm. Tanar could spend the day brewing medicines, and Bosha could, I don't know, assassinate the customers. They'd be happy."

Nikys caught a black laugh in her hand too late to stuff it back into her mouth.

And then the cart was turning onto the street, and other peoples' troubles had to make way for her own. The last leg of this mortal relay.

Maybe.

IX

---

*P*EN CRANED HIS neck as they rattled into the small port village of Guza, on the Cedonian shore opposite Limnos. Dusk muffled its streets in shadows. The sea remained luminous; four miles out, the island bulked as a mysterious silhouette against the horizon. Guza earned much of its living serving Limnos, its Order, and the steady stream of pilgrims making their way to its sacred well. Spring was the busy season for such travelers, but the clear skies and calm waters of summer drew a second wave. In the grimmer winds of winter, Bosha had told them, such traffic shut down.

A hospice of the Daughter's Order in Guza was devoted to housing pilgrims, with a reputation for being the cleanest, cheapest, and safest place to stay overnight. Pen was not willing to test his disguise in the close confines of a women's dormitory, however, where the goddess might not be the sole one to take vigorous offense if he slipped up. Bosha dropped them instead at the inn that was not the mainstay of the sailors, and went off to find secure stabling for Lady Xarre's horse and cart.

Pen had hoped to find separate rooms for all three of them, but was lucky to get even one. The chamber in the eaves held a bed and a straw-stuffed pallet brought-in which, between them, filled the floor. Ruchia advised him to take the offer of plain cold food and drink carried up by a maid in place of a trip to the taproom, and Nikys seemed relieved to go along with this. When Bosha arrived, they made a picnic of it. Pen suspected the retainer dined at home as finely as his mistresses and often with them, but he made no comment on the simplicity of this meal.

Then came the problem of apportioning beds, which brought back memories of the flight to Orbas with Adelis. Nikys, both practiced at the arguments and plainly very, very tired of them, took over, bluntly assigning herself to the pallet and the two men to the bed.

"And don't stare at me like a pair of five-year-olds told to eat their vegetables," she added tartly, blocking protest. Fortunately, Bosha seemed used to following the orders of irate women. It would have made for the most awkward night's sleep imaginable, if Pen hadn't been so fatigued he dropped like a log within moments of hitting the sheets.

He'd no idea of how Bosha had fared, come dawn. The man's eyes were always red.

THE SMALL boats that ferried travelers out to the island left Guza as early as they could make up a passenger list. Several of the captains and crews were themselves women, much favored by some of the pilgrims. Bosha directed them aboard one of these not because he knew it, he said, but because he didn't, and vice versa. As soon as the craft cast off, he clambered over the barrels and crates to crouch in the shadow of the sail, augmented by a wide-brimmed hat that he pulled down over his flushed face.

The little fleet sailed out in the morning and back at dusk, giving their supercargo as long a day as possible to visit ashore. Some pilgrims stayed over, either at the fishing village that served the Order, or at the upper hamlet that lay outside its precincts, and a very few, by arrangement, within the walls, most of the latter being themselves Temple functionaries. Pen kept peeking over the green spectacles to take in as much of the glorious sea light as he could, until Nikys appeared with a straw hat she'd found somewhere, jammed it over his head declaring he was going to fry like an egg, and made him join Bosha in the shade.

They had each supplied themselves with a thin blue scarf, conveniently for sale at a booth on the Guza wharf, marking them as supplicants. Bosha had draped his over his head, secured by his hat and pulled down over his face. He raised this curtain to frown briefly at Pen, then let it drop back. With every inch of skin covered with, mostly, dark cloth, including gloves, he looked hot and very uncomfortable.

"Would you like your spectacles for a while?" murmured Pen.

"No," he muttered back. "If you're going to carry out this play, stay in your character."

He's right about that, said Des.

"I didn't realize this would be such an ordeal for you." The brilliant morning sun reflecting off the sea would have bathed the man in burns, uncovered.

Pen wasn't sure how well Tanar's dye would protect him, either.

"My sister's birthday is in late fall. It's not usually this bad, then."

Nikys sat down on Pen's other side. She seemed to be growing tenser the closer they drew to their goal. Pen nudged her in an attempt at silent reassurance, barely acknowledged by a lip-twitch that did not linger.

With a few barked orders, the boat came about. The sail slid aside like a screen, giving their first view of the Daughter's retreat on Limnos.

Pen looked up. And up. And up. His jaw unhinged. "Five gods preserve me," he breathed.

From the sea, a nearly sheer rock face soared so high into the air that the gray stone buildings atop, roofed with faded blue tile, looked like architect's models. The precipice stood out from the island like the column of a giant's temple.

"That has to be a thousand feet up," Pen marveled.

"Just about that," said Bosha, raising his scarf again to follow Pen's gaze.

"How do people get *up* there?"

"There is a stairway cut into the cliff that winds up it in switchbacks. You'll be able to make it out when we get closer. Over two thousand steps, and every step a prayer."

"A curse, surely, by the end!" said Pen, appalled.

Bosha let him dwell in his horror for a long moment, then added airily, "Or you could pay a coin to the donkey drivers to take you up the road from the village."

Pen, well taken-in, shot him a glare.

The smirk curled back on teeth. "Some rare persons on a pilgrimage of atonement do climb the stairs, I'm told. On their hands and knees. This is less an act of humility than terror, as there are no railings. There are places so narrow that people coming up and people coming down have to crawl over each other."

"I believe we will take the donkeys," said Nikys primly.

"Good decision."

"I'm not sure how such wild feats are supposed to impress the gods," mused Pen, squinting upward, "who are present everywhere the same. Though my subtler seminary teachers advised me that any useful effect is upon the supplicant, not some holy audience. It's all in whether the given action fills a person or empties them, leaving room for a god to enter. You could sit by yourself in a quiet room and have as good a chance at it. A man could walk up those two thousand steps on his hands singing hymns the whole way and have none."

Bosha eyed him curiously. "Could you have such a chance? Learned divine as you apparently are."

"No. Sorcerers are always too full." Pen sighed. "It's all indirection, for my god and me. Maddeningly so, sometimes."

So far up, trees looked like bits of parsley set around a roast. It took study, counting the rows of windows and filigree of wooden balconies, to realize how large the buildings actually were, rising six or eight floors high above the rock base on this side.

"I'm surprised it hasn't been seized for an imperial fortress," said Pen.

"It was, once," said Bosha. "Although not by Cedonia. By one of its enemies. Two hundred years ago. A long tapestry tells the story, up in the halls, that all the pilgrims to Limnos go view."

"So what is the tale?" asked Pen.

"Ah. The ravine was bridged by ladders, and the Daughter's women suffered the usual rapine, slaughter, and carrying-off into slavery. About a week after, the entire garrison was felled by plague.

Of a thousand men, there were only thirteen survivors. It was considered a miracle of the Daughter, in vengeance for the affront. The Order has never been attacked since."

Nikys hummed. "Or a very, very angry woman poisoning the sacred well."

The lip-scar stretched. "So I would make it."

"No reason it can't be both," said Pen, judiciously. "And every reason it could. The gods have no hands but ours, they say." He held up his fingers and wiggled them.

"Not mine," growled Bosha, and retreated back under his blue curtain.

X

S THEIR BOAT took its turn at the Limnos dock and the passengers wobbled their way to shore, Nikys wasn't sure if she was heartsick, homesick, or seasick. Or all of them. The tension in her shoulders made her feel like a plaster statue whose head could crack away at a careless knock. As her feet found the grainy cobblestones, she took a deep breath.

Penric-as-Ruchia captured her hand and gripped it. "Hey," he murmured. "It will be very well."

There was no rational reason at all to believe that. Sorcerers, as far as she knew, didn't possess the powers of seers. But she stretched her neck a little without her head coming off.

Bosha took care to exit the boat apart from them, but it was easy enough to follow the handful of other pilgrims straggling up through the village to the donkey livery. They ducked around the side of the last whitewashed house and handed off their luggage to him, barring one sack containing Mira's clogs, Pen's tunic and trousers, and a packed lunch atop not just for concealment.

"Where will you wait for us?" asked Nikys. "I only saw the one tavern."

"Not there," said Bosha. "Too many people would notice me. A little way up there's a path, and some crevices in the rocks. I'll just evict the adders, and I'll have a dark, cool place to wait out the sun. I should be able to mark you coming back down."

"This island has adders?" said Nikys nervously. She might have taken this for more of Bosha's sly humor, but he was the only one among them wearing boots.

"Not on the road." He smirked, probably. It was hard to be sure. "Your sorcerer will doubtless protect you. ...Animals like him, he tells me."

Ignoring this edged dig, Pen drew her off.

"But who will protect him?" Nikys worried, glancing back over her shoulder. The man had already disappeared.

"From the adders? They'll probably welcome him as a cousin. Given the inventory of tainted blades he's carrying."

"He drugs his belt-knife?"

"Oh, that one's clean. But there's one around his neck, one at his back, one in his boot, and that pouch at his belt is full of nasty little larding-needles."

Nikys considered this. "Good."

"Livery" was perhaps too grand a name for what proved to be a collection of animals tethered in the shade of some olive trees, together with a few rowdy boys for groom-guides, and an adult couple who collected the coins from the pilgrims and portioned out the mounts. The poorer or more fit travelers simply walked up the winding road, although there was also a cart for the aged or infirm. They endured a short delay while a longer-legged donkey was found for the very tall woman with the weak eyes, but soon both Pen and Nikys clambered aboard sidewise saddles like little wooden seats, arranged their skirts, and lurched off towed by a lad.

The road bent back and forth across the sparse hillside like a shuttle on a loom, covering what might have been two miles in a straight line, and a thousand vertical feet. The view across the strait to the mainland of Cedonia was superb, sky and sea a vibrant clear blue that reminded Nikys of Pen's eyes, the land aglow with white light. It only seemed forever before they rounded the last turn and approached the hamlet outside the walls of the Daughter's Order.

She searched for any signs of guards they would somehow have to circumvent, later. A few men in blue tunics of the Order were about, bearing weapons, and under a plane tree four bored soldiers in imperial uniforms played at dice. They paused to look over the latest arrivals to be unloaded, but, after the first flicker of attention, their interest seemed more lewd than suspicious.

Truly, even were he mad enough to do so, it was far too early for Adelis to be arriving with any sort of attack force. Which the sentinels could watch coming up the road long before it arrived.

Except Adelis wouldn't march up the hill in broad daylight. He'd land his troop on the far side of the island in the dark and infiltrate by surprise. So perhaps the soldiers' present relaxation was justified.

The long drawbridge lay down across a plunging cleft, cool and green in its shadowy depths. Nikys gripped Pen's elbow as if assisting her friend while they waited for a blue-clad man to push a cart holding a barrel across, handing it off at the stone archway to a waiting woman. They exchanged brief Daughter's salutes, a tap to the forehead, as well as the load. Nikys and Pen followed it inside.

The forecourt was sunny, paved with interlaced tiles in blue, white, and yellow. On the other side stood a podium womaned by an acolyte wearing a blue scarf, smiling welcome at the visitors and waiting to assist them in signing the guest book, a large ledger. The only hazard was the startling pack of perhaps a dozen guard dogs.

Nikys had vaguely expected something like the Xarre mastiffs, huge and threatening. Instead, these were small beasts, their long coats beautifully brushed, with bright black eyes and pink tongues. It was like being swarmed by a throng of white silk floor mops.

Pen made a faint *urk* sound, and acquired a look of concentration. The dogs' suspicion turned to joy as they rioted around him, snuffling and panting. A couple of them darted in to lick his ankles. Producing a credible feminine *eep*, not wholly feigned, Pen shook his skirts and attempted to gently shove them away with a long sandaled foot. Which would have been all right had their pink tongues not come away with a distinct brown tint. Nikys swallowed horror and bent to them, waving her arms and hissing, "Shoo. Shoo!" They tried to lick her fingers.

To Nikys's intense relief, a woman came in behind them shepherding four young girls, who squealed at their canine reception. Girls and dogs fell upon each other with equal delight, exchanging petting and cooing for licks and wriggles, and Pen escaped.

As planned, Nikys signed in for the both of them, her false name and his, so that there would be no discrepancy in handwriting when it came time to sign out. Assuming anyone actually compared such things. *They will later on, when they discover Mother missing.*

"And what do you pray to our Lady for today?" the acolyte asked cheerfully.

"Oh, nothing for myself. My friend Ruchia is praying for aid for her weak eyes. I'm just here to help her."

Pen nodded amiably, and, by whatever restraint— maybe Des—managed not to add any rambling comments. He pulled a handkerchief from his sleeve and pressed it to his nose just in time to dam the beginning trickle of blood.

"Oh dear, are you all right?" said the acolyte. "Do you need to go sit down?"

Pen shook his head, emitting a muffled negative noise. "S'tops in a mom'nt."

Reluctantly, the acolyte released them to the first stage of the pilgrims' tour, pointing out the entry to the tapestry gallery. Nikys fished out her coin purse and withdrew an offering for the box set up next to the podium, turning her hand to make sure the acolyte caught the heavy gold glint. The acolyte was all smiles as she sent them on their way, though she added a recommendation to the tall girl to return if she felt unwell and someone would guide her to the infirmary.

The famous tapestry was arranged on a long wall, with a series of arched windows opposite that illuminated without allowing direct sunlight to fade it. Penric actually took the time to look at it all, strolling slowly through thirty feet of closely embroidered narrative, murmuring interpretations under his breath. Nikys wasn't sure if he was just doing an excellent job of playing a pilgrim, or if he was overcome with scholarly distraction, again.

One could make out views of the soldiers landing in the fishing cove below, ravaging through something very like the present village. Scaling ladders and smoke. Women screaming, captured by the hair by what appeared to be brutal ogres. A picture of the sacred well, with the goddess looming over it crying in dismay. Her face was portrayed so vaguely as to be a near-blank, because the Nominalist Controversy had taken some vicious turns in Cedonia, but what could be seen of Her posture somehow conveyed profound emotion. Toward the end, many detailed little ogre figures writhed in visible agony and vomited red threads. Lots of red threads.

"I didn't know needlework could be so hostile," murmured Pen, bending to examine these. "Definitely a sermon, there." He licked his lips a touch nervously.

The last image was of the goddess smiling benignly, presiding over billowing smoke from pyres and the restoration of Her refuge. Pen contemplated this and signed himself, hand passing over his forehead for the Daughter, lips for the Bastard, navel for the Mother, groin for the Father, and heart for the Son, bowing slightly and giving his forehead an extra tap.

Then twice with the back of his thumb on his lips for the luck of his own god, however ambiguous.

Because Penric never seemed to forget, though others did, that his powers were lent ultimately by the white god, to Whom he must someday render up an account.

It was an unexpected insight, and Nikys eyed him sideways. She had met him first as physician, then as sorcerer, but he was equally, it seemed, a learned divine. Maybe she hadn't given enough credence to this third pillar of his character.

The gallery let them out down some bluish granite steps into the court of the sacred well, recognizable from the tapestry. But so much more stunning in reality. She and Pen both stopped short and gawped.

From the middle of a white marble circle some eight feet in diameter bubbled up clear, bright waters. *Welling* indeed. Through five ports, it spilled over into an encircling basin. From there, channels led away variously into the surrounding precincts, doubtless including baths and laundries. One spout emptied into a sink with silver ladles hung around it. From there it trickled into something resembling a marble laundry trough, beautifully carved with emblems of the goddess, in which a pilgrim seeking more complete consolation could immerse her whole body.

The music of the waters was the only sound in the hushed court, apart from distant bird-calls. It seemed strange that so glaringly bright a place could feel holy, but it did.

"How," muttered Pen through his teeth, "does the water get *up* here?"

Another acolyte, attendant and guardian-on-duty of the waters, rose from a porphyry bench under a portico and cordially came forward. "We consider it a miracle of the Lady. Four hundred years ago, this place was nothing but a dry and desolate crag. The spring appeared following an earthquake. The inhabitants of Limnos noticed a new waterfall appearing over the side of the pinnacle, and came to investigate. We have celebrated the blessings of the Daughter of Spring here ever since." The wave of an inviting hand. "Drink, then, if you come in good faith, and pray with Her cleansing waters on your lips." Her gesture went on to encompass an array of intricately woven prayer rugs set beyond the well. An older woman, the blue scarf about her neck, was just lumbering up from one, a thoughtful expression on her face.

Nikys took the ladle that was extended and hesitated. The attendant, eyes twinkling, murmured behind her hand, "After the boats and that climb up the hill, most visitors are very thirsty. It's permitted to drink your fill."

Smiling thanks, she did so. Penric watched her cautiously. Moved by impulse, she dipped her ladle and handed it to him. He received it with a grateful nod, and again when she refilled it.

They both wiped their mouths, then proceeded to the prayer rugs, because the attendant was watching them in expectation. Penric, after a contemplative moment, went down not just on his knees but prone, arms wide in the attitude of utmost supplication. Nikys went down on her knees facing the bright fountain and held up her hands palm-out, five fingers spread wide.

For all her anxieties, she had not thought of what to pray. She had nothing.

With the Daughter's water still on her lips, it seemed wrong to perform some dissembling dumb-show. One didn't need to be a virgin to pray here, after all, merely to have once been one. *Because the gods are parsimonious.*

And, sometimes, merciful.

She considered offering the goddess an apology for this sacrilegious invasion. Could they buy dispensation by coming to remove what was certainly a greater insult, using Her shrine for a prison?

...*No.* This was the goddess, not Duke Jurgo. Nikys wasn't here to bargain for something to which she had no native right, trading favors. The court of the sacred well wasn't a marketplace. There was no way to put a value on what she sought.

And no need, child.

Nikys trembled, not sure whose thought that was.

Lady. I do not sin against You, and no forgiveness is required. I am here to do today exactly what a daughter ought. I lay my actions as an offering at Your feet, because we should give to the gods the very best of what is in us.

There is no offense to You in me.

And she knew it to be true.

Penric sighed, rolled over, and sat up, then looked alarmed. "Why are you crying?" he whispered.

"Am I?" said Nikys. She wiped at her cheeks to find them wet. *Daughter's waters, given back.* Her head, and heart, felt overfull in a very different way than before. "It's all right."

"I can take—"

She reached out and caught his hand, laid a finger to stop his anxious lips. "No. It's really all right.

We can go, now." She echoed his own words back to him. "It will be very well." This time, she stood first, and pulled him up after her.

XI

DES WAS CRYING, too. Pen was surrounded, inside and out, by crying women. It was appalling.

His demon's response at least was familiar from their previous sidewise encounters with something like this. *Or Someone like this.* Demons were terrified of gods, the one power that could destroy them. Des's shaking was simple fear. Or maybe not-so-simple fear. Interestingly, she wasn't curled in as tight a ball within him as usual. If she'd had a body other than his own, he'd have imagined her prone, arms out hugging the floor tiles, face turned away, all abject surrender.

Nikys…was something else altogether. Whatever it was, it didn't include a speck of fear. Which was unnerving in its own right.

She wasn't gulping or sobbing or shaking, but water still trickled in fine silver rivulets from the corners of her dark eyes. Anxiously, he drew her away to a bench in the shade of a colonnade, as far as they could get from the well and its attendant. The acolyte was watching them with a curious frown, but then her attention was drawn away by the entry of the woman with the four daughters, still overexcited from their happy encounter with the dogs.

He extended his arm around Nikys's shoulders, hovering tentatively, offering consolation if she wished it. She must have wished something, because she dove into his embrace, her hands going out to grip his draperies. It was not so much a gesture of affection as of drowning. "Whatever did you pray to the goddess to grant?" Pen whispered.

"Nothing." She shook her head. "I made an offering. I suppose."

The five functions of prayer, Pen had been taught, were service, supplication, gratitude, divination, and atonement, of which supplication and divination were the most begged and the least answered. Atonement grew in importance as one moved through life. So what song of service or gratitude was this?

"What did you feel?"

"I can't say."

"Too difficult? Or too private?"

"Both." She looked away. "I can't make claims. Putting myself forward. It might have just been heatstroke."

Pen felt her forehead, then his own. Each were equally warm in this bright day, and he spared a hope that Bosha had found a nice deep crevice. "As I once said to a man who'd had a similar experience: Do not deny the gods. And they will not deny you."

She raised her face, lips parting in surprise. "You believe me?"

"I don't have to believe. I know. Or rather, Des saw. She's almost spasming inside me right now. She'll recover in a while. She does that."

Gazing at him in consternation, she said, "You've encountered something like this before?"

"Three times. One does not forget."

She mumbled into his bodice, "It was surely no more than the brush of the hem of Her cloak."

"Mm, but it's a very great cloak. It covers the width of the world." He sighed. "Or so I imagine.

The most I will ever get is a waft from the flutter of the hem in passing." As now?

Her look grew a trifle wild-eyed. "You understand this?"

"Understand?" He snorted. "As much as I might drink the sea." Envy?...maybe.

She swallowed, and got out, "What did you pray for?"

"It was groveling. Mostly. Lots and lots of groveling. That tapestry is downright menacing."

She tried to choke down her laugh and ended up snorting it through her nose. "You shouldn't...I shouldn't..."

"Yes, you should. Joy is a mark of Them, you see. It will likely keep leaking out of you for some while."

"Oh..." She took a breath, sat up, reordered herself. "And you deal with this sort of thing all the time?"

"Not all the time, white god forfend. Very rarely. I would not survive the overload."

"Why are you still sane?" Her lips pursed, then sneaked up. "Oh. Maybe I answered my own question."

"Now, now. Be nice." He couldn't help it; her grin was infectious. He reached out and lightly brushed the last of the silver from her soft cheeks with the backs of his knuckles. He did not blot the cool away. He tried not to feel like a greedy child snitching a treat from his sister's plate.

Maybe not greedy. Maybe just hungry.

The both gazed out at the court. The four girls had been dissuaded from trying to swim around the annular basin like the line of dolphins that decorated it, but were being permitted to wade and splash in the trough, skirts hiked up, shrieking. There wouldn't be a dry stitch on them, presently. Sandals were strewn everywhere. The acolyte and their mother looked on laughing.

"You know," said Nikys, "I had worked out an elaborate ruse about asking the way to the garderobe, but I don't think it will be needed. Let's just go."

"Aye."

She seemed to find it very natural to twine her arm through that of her tall friend as they quietly moved into the shadowy interior of the next building.

"Where should we look first?" said Pen.

"You're asking me? The goddess didn't exactly give me a map."

"Ah, They never do," sighed Pen. "It's practically another mark."

She finally dared to say it out loud, if very quietly: "...I think She gave me a blessing."

His lips curved up. "Even better."

She seemed to take this in, all the way, for after a breath she nodded. Then said, "So did you have a plan?"

He wrinkled his nose in doubt as they stopped and looked around the next small courtyard. "Bosha thought they'd keep your mother on the side toward the sea, where the drop is most difficult. The top four or five floors have balconies, giving potential access. Or egress. So less likely those. I'd say start on the bottom floor on the east side. Poke around, see what we find."

"What if we're stopped?"

The place was far from unpeopled, although the women they glimpsed all seemed to be hurrying about their business, with scant attention given to the pair of pilgrims not yet too far out of place. "Keep that garderobe story in reserve. It may not be a waste of invention after all."

When they came to the dimmer interior corridors, Pen shoved the green spectacles up on his head under the fold of his drapery. "I shall be glad to be rid of these. Give them back to Bosha if you can. Though not before you reach the boat."

"Of course. I hope he's all right."

After two false casts, they came to a promising stairway. Pen knew they were going the right way when the descent through fine masonry changed to one carved through solid rock. At the very bottom, the stairs turned out onto a long corridor.

On its right side, a few niches reflected an aqueous blue daylight into the corridor. A gallery of near-identical doors lay along it. The left was lined with windowless cells, some with doors across, some open, all apparently used for storage. A scattering of wall sconces were frugally unlit.

"How do we find the right door?" whispered Nikys.

"Hers will be locked, with one person behind it, most likely. If it's unlocked or no one is home, then not." Or so he hoped. *Des, I need you. Rise and shine, love.*

Reluctantly, his demon unfolded within him, still surly from her fright. *Cajoler,* she muttered, but lent him her powers. The first door on their right was both locked and unpeopled, so he opened it to scout the terrain.

As he'd guessed, it was a dormitory cell for lay dedicats. Two narrow beds, simple furnishings, an upright loom against one wall with a colorful prayer rug in progress. A small window through two feet of solid rock gave a fine sea view, and a draught of pure air. Cool, serene. Less delightful in the winter, no doubt. Significantly, no area for the preparation of food.

"The dedicats must take their meals in a common refectory somewhere," he whispered to Nikys. "Suggests your mother's may be brought to her."

He locked up after them, then ran a survey of the rest of the doors, which numbered fifteen.

"There are three doors both locked and with someone inside," he muttered to Nikys. He pointed them out. "Could be dedicats ill, or resting up for night duties. You pick."

"Me!"

"Yes."

She huffed in doubt, walked up to one, hesitated, then moved to the next. "Try here."

He didn't insult her by asking *Are you sure?* She had as good a chance at guessing as he did, and maybe better. But as he unlocked the door, swung it open, and shepherded her in ahead of him, he braced for a cry of *Oh, dear, this isn't the garderobe, sorry!* and a quick retreat.

It only got as far as "Oh—!" before she broke from him and sprinted forward.

Pen came after and eased the door closed. "Keep your voices down," he warned.

A woman lying on a cot turned toward them. Her face was first weary, then wild, as she rolled to her feet and held out her arms in time to receive the pelting Nikys.

"Oh, gods, Nikys! Did they take you, too? I thought you were safely in Orbas! Oh, gods, no…" The mutual embraces held power beyond the mere grip of them, and Pen stood witness in shy silence. No such reunion would ever be his again, his own mother being three years in the cold ground of a country that scarcely still seemed home. Tears started in Nikys's eyes, if not the same as before. Or maybe more closely related than Pen thought.

"No, no, I'm not a prisoner," Nikys gasped into her mother's ear, both women's sets of hands frantically feeling up and down as if to assure their owners of the other's life, health, hope. "We've come to get you out of here."

"What?" Idrene stood back, though not letting go of her daughter's shoulders.

Penric smiled and advanced, feeling dimly that the first thing a man said to his intended's respected mother probably shouldn't be *Quick, take your clothes off!* "I am so pleased to meet you, Madame Gardiki. I'm"—he hastily dumped every confusing and irrelevant honorific—"Nikys's friend Penric."

Nikys looked at him. "Yes," she said. "You are."

Madame Gardiki gave him an utterly baffled smile, reminding him of the false cordiality they'd offered to the Xarre mastiffs, as he laid the spectacles on the washstand, tossed his sack on the bed, shrugged down his draperies, and undid the blue scarf around his neck.

"Plan is you are to exchange clothes with me. You go with Nikys. Two pilgrims enter, two pilgrims leave. I stay in your cell and pretend to be you for as long as I can."

"But how do you get out?"

"I have a scheme."

No, you don't, scoffed Des. *It's all improvisation from here.*

"He'll manage, Mother," said Nikys. He hoped that heartening confidence wasn't feigned.

"He?...Oh." She stepped back a pace as he continued to disrobe, pulling off his belt and shucking the dress up over his head. With Ruchia's loose, demure clothing, they hadn't bothered with stuffing a breast-band. He was down to his trews when he realized what a bizarre figure he must present. Sky-blue eyes glittering out of a ruddy face, black bun on his nape, chest hair a smattering of gold, piebald with richly colored arms and shins but thighs and torso milk white.

Nikys, thankfully, took over the task of coaxing Idrene out of her own clothes. "It's all right, Mother, Pen's a physician."

"Yes, and I'm an army wife, but I've never seen anything like *that*." She seemed to have grasped the escape scheme at once; her distraction was all for Pen. "A physician, really? He seems too young."

"I'm almost thirty-one," Pen told her, waiting to pass along his garments. His torso was narrower than hers, and longer, but Cedonian styles were forgiving. Nikys excavated down to her mother's shift and tossed her dress his way, taking Ruchia's in trade.

Given Idrene Gardiki's still-handsome appearance at fifty, she must have been stunning at twenty. No wonder the old general had been beguiled. Not to mention young officer Rodoa before him. Her loose black hair had a mere smattering of gray in it, and Pen had kept his draperies over his head throughout, so that substitution shouldn't be a problem. It would only take a moment to wind a similar bun. At least they'd matched her skin. Her features were sharper than Nikys's, if not much like Pen's, but the green spectacles would hide a lot. The bodice of Ruchia's dress would be better-filled, but not unduly so. The clogs would still leave her wanting an inch or two of height, but if they avoided the two welcoming acolytes on the way out, and chanced a different donkey-lad for the trip down, she should pass. Pen had made sure to speak as little as possible. *Check, check, check...*

"Tell me what your daily routine has been in here, Madame Gardiki. I must know what to expect."

"Fear and boredom, mostly. I've been here three weeks—I've been scratching the days on the wall down out of sight behind the bed. Five gods, dear Nikys, how did you get here so fast?"

"We had help. You'll meet some of it in a bit. I'll tell you all the rest later."

"Do they carry in your meals on a tray?" asked Pen. "Who brings it?"

Idrene nodded. "Yes, three times a day. They haven't been starving me, except of news. I'd only just heard, at home, that Adelis had been arrested in Patos, and—dear Mother's mercy, was he really blinded? Because the men who came to arrest me said he'd fled to Orbas, and there was no word of you at all, and *nothing* made sense." Nikys guided Ruchia's dress over her head. "Darling, I'm going to trip on this hem."

"No, we brought shoes. Keep going."

She shoved her arms through the wide sleeves, and went on, "A dedicat brings the tray, but there are always these two large women with her who aren't of the Order. None of them talk to me, though I think the dedicat is curious."

"Always the same women?" said Pen.

"Usually."

"So they'd recognize I wasn't you if they saw me closely?"

"Yes, probably..." She eyed him as he adjusted her belt around his waist. "Yes. Although you make a convincing woman in general."

"I've had practice." Pen grimaced. "How soon are they due back?"

"Sunset."

"You two should be almost back to Guza by then. I might be able to fake my way through one meal. Maybe more."

"How will you catch up with us? Where will you catch up with us?" said Nikys, a distraught edge leaking into her voice.

"Akylaxio, I hope." A larger seaport up the Cedonian coast from Guza. "But if Bosha can find you what seems a good safe ship there heading north, don't wait for me. Keep going. It might be as late as Orbas."

"We're going to Orbas?" said Idrene faintly.

"Yes, Adelis has taken service with Duke Jurgo," said Nikys.

"He's better? But what—" She broke off as Nikys started yanking her hair into a bun.

"His eyesight is restored, though his face is scarred."

"That hardly seems possible."

"It was magical."

"Yes, but—"

"I mean actually magical. Pen is a sorcerer as well as a physician." She added as he opened his mouth to object, "In all but final oath."

Idrene rolled her eyes toward Pen. "Wherever did you find him?"

"He found us. Long story, which I will tell you *later.*" She made her mother sit on the cot, and knelt to fit the raised clogs.

"Oh, mustn't forget this," said Pen, drawing the thong of his coin purse over his head. He advanced to fit it over Madame Gardiki's, and she cast him up a look of surprise, fingering the leather bag and testing its heavy weight in her palm. "If you should get separated from Nikys, gods forbid, you shouldn't be without resources."

"But what will you have?"

"I've a coin belt around my waist." The narrow cloth band held the rest of Duke Jurgo's largess. "Nikys has another. We did come prepared." And what a huge difference that had made, although it helped that they had not been sucked dry by need for bribes. Yet. "Might be wise to hide the thong under your scarf. I did." He handed her the blue cloth, which she draped around her neck, tucking the purse in her bodice.

At last the dual transformation was completed. Nikys walked around her mother. "That's not bad, really." She frowned at Pen. "She can pass as you, at a distance. I'm not so sure you can pass as her."

"That is not your problem. You have enough on your plate. Get yourselves to Orbas before Methani even knows you're gone."

"Oh, you think it was old Methani behind all this?" said Idrene, eyes narrowing behind the green spectacles. "Plausible."

Pen herded them both toward the door. "Madame Gardiki, so good to have met you. I trust I will see you again soon."

She made a vague protesting noise, then threw up her hands, muttering, " 'Over the wall, boys, follow me.' *Yet again.*" Plainly a quote of some personal significance. He hoped he'd get its story later.

Nikys stopped in front of Pen, glowering up at him. She bit her lip. Drew breath. "I absolutely forbid you to get yourself killed, either, you know."

Was that how a woman said *I love you* without saying *I love you?* Pen thought it must be so.

He grinned and touched his hand to his heart, echoing her echo. Then tapped her lips twice with his thumb, for whatever blessing he could muster. "Our god guard you on your way. And the rest of His kin."

When he closed and locked the door behind them, the cell felt very silent and empty.

XII

S SHE GUIDED her mother into the dim blue corridor, the goddess's blessing still seemed to bubble in Nikys's veins like some fizzy wine. The elated confidence in which it cloaked her should not become overconfidence, she reminded herself sternly, because that would be to take more than was offered. She still had to control an irrational urge to smile.

Idrene pulled the green spectacles down her nose and peered over them. "How does he see in these things?"

"They will be better outside, which is where they are intended to be used," Nikys whispered back. "Although Pen can also see in the dark. One of his handier skills."

Idrene glanced back to her door at click of its lock latching, apparently by itself. "I must hear more about that strange young man."

"You shall," Nikys promised with certainty, "when we get to a place we can talk. For now, don't speak to anyone if you can avoid it. Don't rush and don't linger. Pen said—or maybe it was Ruchia—we should move as though we had bespoken dinner in the village tavern, and didn't want to be late."

Idrene nodded. "Who's Ruch—never mind. Later."

Nikys led back the way they had come in, minus the wrong turns. In the court of the sacred well, a last few pilgrims had arrived and were occupying the attendant's attention. The only signs of the woman with the four daughters were the puddles left around the trough, drying more slowly as the afternoon shadows moved across the tiles. They sped past the tapestry in reverse order. Idrene eyed it sideways, reaching out for a bare touch. "Hm. Maybe it's as well it wasn't Adelis to come to my rescue."

In the forecourt, while Nikys signed them out in the ledger, the silky dogs sniffed Idrene indifferently.

Nikys received many tickling licks on her sandaled feet. She wasn't sure if it was for Pen's lingering geas or some scent of the goddess, but the dogs whined in disappointment as she left.

Then across the drawbridge, under the benign eyes of the armed male dedicats guarding it. This wasn't the end of their escape, Nikys reminded herself, just the first stage, though Idrene vented a long exhalation as they stepped onto the gravel.

Nikys made straight for the top depot of the donkey livery. As they were led down the winding road once more, Idrene adjusted her spectacles and stared around, concealing tension. The time it took to descend the hill seemed unnaturally longer than it had taken to ascend. Doubtless an illusion. The whole east side of the island lay in its own shadow by the time they found Bosha, sitting with their luggage in the lee of the same house as before.

He rose as they approached and gave them a polite bow, though his hand did not touch his heart. Apparently that enigmatic gesture was reserved for Tanar and Lady Xarre.

As Idrene stopped warily, blinking, as one tended to do at first sight of the albino's singular features, Nikys hurried to introduce them. "Mother, this is Master Surakos Bosha, Lady Tanar's secretary. He's been helping us, by the kind courtesy of Lady Xarre."

"Madame Gardiki. A pleasure." The light voice was smoothly cultured, and Nikys wondered again at his origins.

"Oh." Her mother relaxed, returning a nod. "Yes, I see! A few of Adelis's letters from Thasalon mentioned you, Master Bosha." She added aside to Nikys, "Not that he wrote that often. I'm sure his fingers weren't broken, though in that case he could still have dictated something to a scribe."

"I know he wrote you from Patos. I made him."

"Ah, that accounts for it. Thank you, dear."

Bosha glanced up the hill toward the just-visible blue roofs of the Order, reflecting the last gleams of sun. How soon would the gaolers be bringing the prisoner's supper? "I suggest we get off Limnos first. All else can follow."

"Yes," agreed Idrene, fervently.

Bosha took charge of their luggage servant-fashion, and they followed him to the dock.

As the boat heeled in the soft evening breeze, they were again surrounded by strangers within earshot. Still no chance to talk. The late afternoon light was warmer in color, but not much of an improvement for Bosha, who pulled down his hat and sought what shade the deck provided. While the crew moved about them, exchanging cheerful calls, and the rigging creaked and the waves slapped, Nikys and Idrene held hands in silence.

Nikys wondered how far the blessing of the goddess extended. Her Order? The island? Or, as Penric had claimed, the width of the world?

With the sea light in her eyes that he so plainly loved, Nikys meditated on Penric. After that overwhelming moment of prayer in the well court, the validation and valediction he had so casually bestowed on her had stunned her almost as much. It was the most outrageous claim she had ever made in her life: to be, however briefly, god-touched.

He believed me.

If he had not...she still would have known. *But he believed me.* It seemed an intimacy strangely deeper than a kiss.

No, better...he *knew*, as she had. She thought she'd plumbed his depths—she could, after all, list every one of his demon's former sorcerous riders by name, in order, and was slowly gathering their biographies, but... What other mysteries did that packed blond head hold? *If you let him sail back to Adria, you'll never find out, now will you?* She sighed.

Aside from one slightly seasick passenger who almost tottered over the gangplank, saved by the conducting sailor-girl, they landed without incident. Nikys looked back at the distant hump of Limnos, dark against the glowing sunset. Had Pen brought off his plan of passing for her mother at dinner, or were the Order's residents just now starting to search for their missing prisoner? And if so, had Pen escaped arrest or not? Firmly, she reminded herself of his victory over the bottle dungeon. The memory didn't help that much.

"Should we take some of that?" asked Idrene, as Bosha hoisted their belongings once more.

"No, Madame. I'm going to fetch the cart. You'll best serve by picking up some food and drink we can eat on the road. Meet me where the south shore road leaves the village." He glanced west. "I'm loth to lose any light we have left." Though full dark would still overtake them long before they reached Akylaxio, and the new moon would be no help. That town was walled, thus the gates would be shut at dark and require some negotiation for admittance, or else a wait till dawn.

The Guza street markets were deserted at this hour, so Nikys returned to the same inn where they'd stayed before. She was made to pay a gallingly stiff price for the basket that she would not be bringing back. Idrene stayed outside on the bench. But the two women wearing the blue scarves and weary demeanors of pilgrims returning after their long day's outing drew few glances.

Bosha arrived at almost the same time as they did where the houses straggled off along the south road. He jumped down and handed them up into the cart. It was a small, light, open vehicle, with an oiled sail-cloth hood that might be raised to protect passengers from the elements, and well-sprung. Bosha, hat now not shielding him from the sun so much as concealing his memorable white hair, played driver with bland assurance, clicking Lady Xarre's well-bred horse into a trot. Nikys and Idrene settled back into the padded rear seat with near-matching huffs of relief.

"I can't believe we're really doing this," said Idrene.

"I've done it before, with Adelis and Penric. I can't say I've become used to it."

Idrene turned to her, the public mask dropping from her urgent face. "Tell me everything that befell you!"

"You first."

"Hah. I imagine that will take less time." Her hand clenched on her knee. "I had no warning, just a troop of imperial soldiers pounding on our door, shouting for admittance. They told me they had an order for my arrest, but didn't even say where I was going. They may not have known. I'd barely time to pack a few necessities and tell off the servants. The boys were reasonably restrained—perhaps your father's shadow daunted them—but they ransacked the house for papers and correspondence. Thank goodness there are copies of my most important documents at the notary's."

"It was the same when the governor's men came to our villa in Patos, after Adelis was arrested at the barracks," said Nikys. "They seized every paper they could find, including all my old letters from Kymis. I was so furious about that. But they didn't steal much, and no one was raped, not even the maidservants. Although most of them quit right after. I couldn't blame them."

Idrene nodded. "I have no idea what's left at home by now. It's been three weeks." She blew out her breath. "Such a bother. I believe if they'd burned the place to the ground, it would be less a burden on my mind."

Nikys, who'd thought her mother would be as hard to extract from the house she'd shared with Florina as a whelk from its shell, was startled at this assertion.

"I wonder if I'll ever get anything back," Idrene went on. "If we're in Orbas for long, the house will surely be stripped, confiscated, and sold." She scowled. "After that, they hauled me out to that island, and then it was three weeks of pacing the cell staring at that sea-moat, and to think I used to like sea views, and no one telling me *anything.* Mend that, I beg you."

Bosha's back was very straight, but Nikys fancied that if he could swivel his ears like the horse, they'd be pointed their way. He had a very good memory, she recalled Tanar bragging.

Nikys began to recount the tale from Adelis's arrest to their arrival in Orbas, in much greater detail than she'd confided to Tanar. It ended up more scrambled than she'd hoped, as her mother kept interrupting with muddling questions that made her lose the thread. She began to have more sympathy for Tanar when she realized that every other name out of her own mouth wasn't *Adelis* either. She glided very lightly over their interlude in Sosie, which had revealed some truly unexpected skills on Penric's part. She dwelt more on the frightening injury he had taken in the uncanny fight with that other sorcerer. Less on how frightening it had been when his magics had brought down *half a hillside*.

"The poor fellow, what a welcome to Cedonia!" Idrene commented. "First he gets his skull cracked, then tossed into a bottle dungeon, then this!"

"He can turn his healing on himself," said Nikys. "Fortunately. Or his demon does. She seems to favor him greatly." Her frequent backtrackings trying to explain Desdemona to her mother were responsible for much of the muddle. Appropriate for a chaos demon, Nikys supposed.

Gleaming reflections from the sea, glimpsed to their right, were keeping the road visible well into the long twilight. Bosha pulled the cart off at a sheltered spot, tended to the horse, then climbed in to sit backward on his seat as Nikys shared out the food and drink from the basket. Idrene made polite inquiries into the healths of Lady Tanar and Lady Xarre, about which Bosha as politely assured her, as though they were sitting down in some gracious dining room.

"I hope I may yet get a chance to meet them, someday," Idrene sighed.

"You would quite like Lady Tanar," said Nikys. "And she, you. I should write when we reach Orbas, to tell her of our safe arrival."

Bosha sat bolt-up. "I would beseech you not to, Madame Khatai! This has all been dangerous enough. Vile suitors I can fend off. I did as much for Lady Xarre, when she first employed me in her early widowhood. The imperial government outmatches me."

Nikys took in the well-hidden implications of that, and slowly swallowed her mouthful of dried apricot. "Surely Lady Xarre's wealth buys some protection?" Or was Bosha the protection that it bought? *No...* She didn't imagine he was underpaid, yet that sort of loyalty wasn't bought with coin, but rather, kind.

Bosha, a trifle self-consciously, eased back. "But it draws down greater dangers. Men may strive to marry a fortune if they can, but are willing to try less pleasing methods to secure it if they can't. A charge of treason, no matter how contrived, makes a fine shield for stripping the accused of his property. Or hers."

"As even my son lately found," Idrene agreed grimly. "And him a general."

"I once thought his rank might be enough to make him safe," said Bosha, "and safe for Lady Tanar, but the events in Patos proved otherwise, if they blinded the man on the basis of one forged letter."

"Learned Penric says he's very sorry about that," Nikys put in. She had been forced to reveal Penric's Adriac origins to her mother, and therefore to the listening Bosha, or there would have been no explaining him at all. "The reply he carried from Adria was in good faith, he claims, but Adelis's enemies had it off him within half an hour of his setting foot in the country. He thinks their agent was watching him the whole time."

"No doubt," said Bosha. "Events have over-turned nearly everything, but with the amount of paper they seized from both your houses, they could have manufactured something just as lethal. When I worked in the Thasalon chancellery, we could have done it with six lines." He chased a bite of cheese with a bite of bread.

Nikys's eyebrows rose. "I didn't know you had served in the imperial bureaucracy."

He shrugged. "Almost eight years. It's not a secret. Although my career was under the reign of the prior emperor, and was truncated when he was."

"And as violently?" inquired Idrene, much interested.

"Only because my father chose to throw in our family's lot with one of the losing pretenders. I might have been able to weather the storm otherwise." He grimaced. "Or had I not let him draw me home when the wrong soldiers arrived. Bad day. I barely escaped with my life." He took a swallow of barley-water. "Cured me of ambition."

Idrene looked as though she had no trouble filling in the horrors he'd left out. Nikys did some mental calculations.

"Was that when you went into Lady Xarre's service?"

"Indirectly. I'd fled the debacle—"

Nikys translated that as *slaughter.*

"—at my family's estate, and ended up taking shelter that night in the Xarre garden. In what turned out to be Lady Tanar's tree house, which was not at all what a boy would have imagined as a tree house. I thought the reason all the furnishings seemed so small was because I was delirious. Which I did become, later on."

He eyed his appreciative female audience hanging on his tale, and unfolded a trifle more. "When Lady Tanar found me there the next day, I begged her to hide me. I'd some dim notion of making it seem like a game to her. She entered into it with more enthusiasm than I quite...quite knew what to do with. Smuggled me food and drink and bandages." He touched the left side of his mouth, which quirked up. "My physician was six, and had never sewn anything but a hem before, but she did her best. I can still picture the charmingly intense look of concentration on her face as she bent over me. Stabbing me repeatedly." His amusement slipped to a grimace. "And my blood up to her wrists. That was disturbing. In retrospect. At the time I had other things on my mind.

"Really, it was the first thing I ever taught her. How to sew up skin. She was a shockingly quick study. It set the tone for our future dealings in a way, hm, that I've never been able to get back under my control since." He looked up, producing an awkward smile. "And that's my one and only war story, in full."

Nikys wagered not. Neither sole nor complete, though evidently pivotal.

"And here I am telling it to the general's widow. You lived through those times. I'm sure you've seen worse."

"No," said Idrene, with a thoughtful look at him. "Merely more."

He hesitated, then inclined his head in delicate appreciation.

"How did you get out of the tree house?" Nikys couldn't help asking.

"Ah. The game couldn't last, of course. After about two weeks I grew so feverish Lady Tanar became frightened enough to ask for help. Of her mother, fortunately for me. I think the servants would have turned me over to the soldiers, or just tossed me into the street. Lady Xarre chose otherwise. I was kept discreetly in her household until I recovered. I found ways to make myself useful, and stayed."

So much so that he was still there fourteen years later?

"Lady Xarre took a risk," Idrene observed. Her tone made it an observation of fact, not a judgment.

Bosha opened his hands. "Time went on, the capital settled back down. I was forgotten soon enough. My family were not great lords. None of my older brothers survived to renew the threat. Nor was I going to start the clan over."

Which was one reason the court bureaucracy favored eunuchs for high posts; they could not put the aggrandizement of their nonexistent children over the needs of the empire. Despite all, the clan game was still played, with families cutting and placing a spare son in such service to later boost brothers or nephews. Nikys wondered if the Boshas had once had some such plan for their odd fifth son. It seemed to have gone profoundly awry, if so.

"My father lived for a while, after. I was glad of that." His crooked lips drew back in a smile that was all sharp edges, like a poisoned blade. "Long enough to know I was his sole remaining son."

He turned about and climbed down from the cart to ready the horse for the next stage.

Which raised another question, which Nikys absolutely could not ask: had Bosha been a *volunteer*, exactly, for his bureaucratic career? Or had he been pressured or forced into it by a family overburdened with sons competing for their inheritances? That, too, happened sometimes.

No, she thought, contemplating his story. *I've no need to ask.*

THE STARLIGHT scintillated overhead as they took the road again, but the deep shadows on the ground slowed them to a walking pace. At times even the earnest carthorse balked, and Bosha would go to its head to lead it, murmuring reassurances in the fuzzy flicking ears. Nikys hoped the pale man's misery in bright light was repaid by better vision at night.

At least they were making steady progress away from Limnos. She hesitated to call it the right direction, as they would have to double back north by ship to circumnavigate the Cedonian peninsula and reach Orbas again. If they had to sail without Penric would there be some safe way to leave him word which ship they'd taken?

Would he be safe at all, or was he being as over-confident as whatever error had led him to that first ugly sojourn in the bottle dungeon? His powers were astonishing, but subtle, and she knew he could be taken by surprise, or overwhelmed by numbers. Her mind's eye went on to produce an unwanted string of vivid playlets of how this might happen, growing more and more horrific and bizarre. And unlikely, she told herself sternly. He would not end up smashed on the rocks, or drowned in the sea, or beaten by brutal soldiers till the blood ran down to flood those blue eyes with opaque red. He had skills. He had tricks. He had Desdemona.

So few people knew how *valuable* that bright blond head was, that was the trouble. How irreplaceable. The notion of him being killed by ruffians wholly ignorant of what they destroyed was the most sickening of all.

She wished her imagination came with a lever to shut it off, like an irrigation gate. This nightmare garden needed no watering.

The darkness was cooling rapidly. Nikys leaned against her mother, who leaned equally exhausted against her, and not just to share heat. As the horse plodded on, Nikys wondered if she had just traded a gold coin for a gold coin.

XIII

*D*ES FELT THE presence of the women in the corridor before Pen heard the key in the lock. Swiftly, he huddled himself up on the cot facing the wall, drapery drawn over his head, simulating a prisoner in deep depression at her fate. Rather as Idrene had looked when they'd first come in, come to think.

He trusted he wouldn't have to attempt a geas. Apart from the challenge of trying to cast it on three subjects at once, the trouble with using a geas on a person—as contrasted with an animal—was that when it wore off, the person *remembered*.

"Madame Gardiki?" The dedicat's voice was not unkind. The other two presences seemed bored but watchful. "Your dinner is here."

Idrene's voice had been a warm alto. Pen lightened his baritone and shoved his face into his pillow. "Just leave it on the table. I'll get to it." And, after a calculatedly reluctant moment, "Thank you."

Rattling and bustle, as they took the old meal tray and left the new one, refilled the pitcher of drinking water, refreshed the ewer on the washstand, swapped out the chamber pot in the discreet commode chair in the corner. Herded back to the doorway. The dedicat's voice, tentatively: "Is there anything else you need tonight, Madame?"

Pen shook his head into his pillow.

"Goddess bless," said the dedicat, and withdrew with her silent outriders.

Oh, She does! thought Pen as the lock clicked over once more. It was the one thing he'd wanted most from this dangerous masquerade: a clear halfday's start for Idrene and Nikys. The attendants would not return till dawn, barring some random bed-check. Should that occur, Des could rust the lock to slow their entry, and he could...well, no. That would trap him on the wrong side of the door. Hiding under the bed was bound to fail, being the first place to search. Cabinets and chests would be as bad, had they existed.

Pen went to the deep window and looked out. In the last level light, a few golden sails hurried toward the harbor of Guza. He wondered if Nikys was aboard one, or if they'd already landed. The specks were much too far away to make out figures aboard.

The window had wooden shutters on this side to close against the drafts. Would parchment or glass be substituted in winter? If not, it would make for a gloomy chamber. The opening was taller than wide. He could not fit in his shoulders square-on, but turning sideways he might slip through easily. Lying along the grainy sill, he put his head out for a survey.

He looked into a wide gulf of air, across the darkening blue strait, and down a dizzying slide of stone to a distant necklace of rocks with the white lace of surf foaming over them. Mountaineer or no, the drop was as appalling as it was awe-inspiring. A thin crinkle might be the lower reaches of the penitential steps. An upper course, hacked into bare rock, still lay sixty feet below his window. He shuddered, and determinedly found another direction to study.

Left and right, he could just make out the apertures of the fourteen other windows cut on this level. No ledges, no handholds to even begin to entice him out. He was secretly relieved. Twisting his neck, he studied the jutting joists and braces of the balconies twenty feet up. A man with a grappling hook and a death wish might make something of that, but he had brought neither.

His escape, when it came, would have to be through the corridor. Somewhere to his left, the precipitous stairway must rise to the level of the buildings and climax at a gate other than the closely guarded, and presently raised, drawbridge. Such a postern was doubtless locked and barred for the night, which was fine from this side even without magic.

That exit would leave him to make his way down all two thousand steps in the moonless night. Never had he been more grateful for Des's dark vision. At least it seemed unlikely he'd have to crawl over any other climbers on the curves.

Feeling heartened to have a clear plan, he washed his hands, sat, and consumed Madame Gardiki's dinner. It was a cut above the seminary food in his old student refectory; probably the same as the ladies of the Order were sitting down to eat together somewhere. The portions could have stood to be a little more generous. A search of the room after he'd cleaned his plate turned up only a small bag of almonds, which he methodically cracked and ate by way of dessert.

There would still be too many women abroad in the precincts to venture out yet. He emptied his own clothes out of his sack and gratefully put them on, then used Madame Gardiki's hairbrush to tidy his still-black hair and tie it into a proper queue. Gathering up her few belongings, he put them in the sack by way of trade. He might have a chance to give them back to her. Her dress he would put back on over his tunic and trousers, to give the proper silhouette to any watchers he might encounter in the darkened halls, later.

That left her shawl. He eyed the window, and thought he might put the wrap to best use by pitching it out to be found on the rocks below. Leaving her gaolers to wonder if they were searching for an escapee, or the body of a suicide carried off by the tide, a theory supported by her still-locked door. That should be good for some splendid misdirection.

Satisfied, Pen drank a couple of glasses of water to assure he wouldn't oversleep past dawn, then lay down on the cot for a restoring nap.

SOMEONE WAS calling him. *Ake...p...ake...up... wake...up!*

Des...?

A heavy hand gripped his shoulder, and Pen froze, mentally scrambling to prepare some burst of action. Or magic. Or both.

About time! cried Des.

And then an anxious male voice murmured, "Mother...?"

...Oh, said Des. *Dear.*

It was not a voice Pen recognized. Certainly not Adelis's. Pen let his snatched-up chaos carefully leak away. Sighed. And said to the wall, "By which I'd guess you must be Ikos Rodoa."

The figure, a black hulk in the darkness, gasped and recoiled. The faint starlight and sea-light glimmering in from the window barely allowed eyes to distinguish shadow from substance, though Pen thought he might have sensed him by the smell, a long workday's worth of dried sweat. *Des, light.*

The colorless clarity of Pen's night-sight sprang forth, revealing a sturdy man with broad shoulders, Cedonian-dark hair, and rounded features that might be pleasant were they not clenched in dismay. The man whipped a blade from his belt, but did not at once attack, possibly because he could not tell Pen's head from his tail in the gloom.

Not quite sure what was going to happen when he remedied that, Pen said, "I'm a friend. Don't cry out," and allowed the pair of candles on the wash-stand to flare to life. The sudden yellow glare seemed searing to dark-adapted eyes, and they both blinked and scrunched their lids against it. The wavering knife blade winked flame.

Why did every Cedonian he met start by trying to stab him? Slowly, Pen rolled over and sat up on the edge of the bed, holding his hands open and still.

"You're not my mother!"

Pen suppressed an acerb reply in favor of efficiency. "Madame Gardiki escaped earlier. Your effort is admirable but a bit late." Wait. The door...the door was still locked. The rush of shock at last cleared the sleep fog from his brain, and he added sharply, "How in five gods' names did you get in here?"

The man pointed mutely at the window.

Pen jerked up and strode to stare out, to be confronted with a confusing mess of cables, pulleys, and a couple of dangling loops that resembled, and may have been, canvas saddle girths. He followed four long ropes upward to where they were apparently hooked to some balcony joists. He didn't look down again, because that would be too unsettling. "Ah," he said, a little thickly. "That's right. You're the bridgebuilder." He drew back inside.

"Who in the Bastard's hell are you?" Ikos demanded.

Or out of it, murmured Des, as intent and perplexed as Pen.

"My name is Penric. I'm...helping Nikys rescue her mother."

The dark eyes flickered at his half-sister's familiar name, if Pen was guessing this right. "Why?"

The simple answer had worked before, and had the advantage of being true. "I'm courting Nikys."

"Oh." Ikos sheathed his knife and raised a large hand to scratch through his mop of short-cut hair. "Time someone did that." His eyes narrowed. "D'you know what's going on? I'd stopped in at Mother's house a few weeks ago. Neighbor said she was arrested, and General Arisaydia blinded in Patos. Why they'd take her if he'd already been blinded made no sense to me, but I followed on and tracked her here. Took me another week to figure how to get her out."

At his expectant look, Pen said, "Adelis's sight recovered, and he and Nikys escaped to Orbas."

"Huh! *That's* a miracle. But that explains. Those idiots at Thasalon court have sure made themselves an enemy now." He nodded shortly.

Pen was rather fascinated by just how fast Ikos connected the political gaps in this complicated tale. But then, he was a Cedonian born and bred.

Ikos frowned around. "Is that water?" He strode to the washstand and drank directly from the pitcher, long gulps, then paused to stare, puzzled, at the candles.

Pen quickly redirected his attention. "When you got Madame Gardiki out"—had he planned to transport her on that terrible contraption, like a timber being raised into place?—"what were you going to do with her?"

"Couldn't take her home, they'd look there. Eventually. Same problem hiding her in my work crew. I figured to send her to some friends in Trigonie. I built a bridge there two years ago."

All right, that was reasonable, although there was a bit of a gap between dangling from a balcony on Limnos to surprising some host in the duchy of Trigonie. It didn't sound much more tenuous than any of Pen's plans. Each of their schemes, it seemed, were sound in their ways. Until they'd run headlong into each other...

And now there was a problem. Two problems.

Ikos evidently felt it, too. Propping his fists on his hips, he looked Pen up and down. "Brother-in-law, eh?"

Pen mentally fitted the term on Ikos in turn, and felt disoriented. "If she'll have me."

"Then I suppose she'd be upset with me if I left you here. Mother'd likely have words, too." He sighed in a very traditional male-put-upon-by-women manner. Possibly not completely sincere. Given the amount of trouble he'd put himself to, unasked, to arrive in this spot.

Pen had one dress between them, and he didn't think it would fit Ikos, shorter and squarer than Penric anyway. Pen would have to use his dark-sight to guide the two of them through the precincts as quickly and quietly as possible, and take a chance on encounters with the residents. Maybe Ikos would have a clue where the stair-postern lay.

"We had better go out together," said Pen.

"Aye," Ikos reluctantly agreed.

Pen started for the door. Ikos started for the window.

They both stopped. "Where're you going?" asked Ikos. He pointed seaward. "Way out's that way."

"You...propose to take us both in your, uh, device?" Des actually screeched: *He's not getting me up in that thing!* Pen winced.

"Why not? I was going to take my mother. It's perfectly safe to twice her weight and mine. I tested it." He rubbed his stubbled jaw. "What's the matter? Got no head for heights?"

"I do reasonably well at them," said Pen, while Des gibbered, *No, no, no!* "But that's a lot of height out there." If it was true a dying man saw his life flash before his eyes, Pen thought that fall might give enough time for all thirteen of his and Des's.

Ikos shrugged. "Way I figure, once a drop is enough to kill you, any more you add makes no difference."

"A reasonable argument."

No it's not, it's insane!

Pen went to take another look at the contraption, and check the clock of the stars. The two girths, he judged, must be intended as seats like bosun's chairs. The succession of pulleys was more complex, the logic of their sequencing not immediately obvious to his untrained eyes. It was certainly an ingenious device.

Des radiated something like murderousness at his open intrigue.

Pen raised his eyes to the horizon to check for any recognizable constellations, and drew a harsh breath. The stars to the east were melting away into the steel gray of dawn. He turned back to the room. "It's much later than I'd thought."

Ikos tilted one hand back and forth. "The stairs were about what I'd calculated, but walking my way across under the balconies took longer than I'd planned. May be faster going back for the practice." He hesitated. "Slower for the added weight."

"I think we'd better try my way."

"Which is what?"

"Sneaking."

Ikos's mouth screwed up in misgiving. "How're you getting out the door?" He paused. "How'd you get in here, for that matter?"

"I'm good with locks."

"Well, so would I be, if I had my tool belt with me. Left it behind for the weight, though." His eyes narrowed at Penric. "How do I know there aren't half-a-dozen guardsmen the other side of that door, waiting for me?"

"There aren't. Yet. Besides, if this were that sort of trap, better to have them on this side of the door. You'd be trussed like a chicken already."

A long, thoughtful silence. "I like my way better."

How was he to persuade Ikos to trust him in three minutes, when three months had not sufficed for his sister Nikys? Pen sucked breath through his teeth. Threw up his hands. "Fine. Your way. So long as it's *now*."

No! cried Des as he crossed the room, wadded up the shawl, and pitched it out, to Ikos's evident bafflement. He reconsidered his sack. If he was staging a convincing suicide, the personal effects would need to be left in place, right. He grabbed it up and circled the room again, putting things back. Shoved the sack and dress under the mattress. "Right, ready—"

The lock rattled. Pen whipped his head around and rusted it stuck before Des could even voice an objection. "We just ran out of time," he whispered. "Go." He held a finger to his lips as thumps sounded on the door.

Ikos oozed sideways through the window. Penric glanced back. On the other side of the door, the sturdier attendant was trying her hand turning the big iron key. Pen ran a hair-thin line of rust through its barrel and grinned as it snapped off in the lock. He was fairly sure the sharp words that resulted, muffled by the door, weren't ones a lady was supposed to say in the Daughter's Order. Or anywhere else.

He added an extra burst of corrosion to guarantee the half-key would stay jammed in the face of anything short of a hammer and chisel, drill, and crowbar. Or an ax.

Ikos's feet kicked and disappeared. Pen eased his torso through, and watched the man, one arm wrapped around a rope or vice versa, bend up and thread his legs through the loop of a girth. He wriggled it under his hips, straightened his spine and shoulders, and braced the other arm over the suspending eye and swivel, and across his chest. He rotated dizzyingly, snaked his hand around the second suspension rope, and swung the girth toward Pen. "Just like that," he whispered. "Then hold still and leave the rest to me. You can't help, and I don't need interference."

Des wailed as Pen copied the procedure. The girth closed up tight around his narrow hips as it took his weight. He clamped both arms around the suspending lines, gripping each other.

It wasn't often that he spoke sharply to his demon, but he did now. *Des, we're committed. Settle down and keep your chaos strictly to yourself until I say otherwise!*

A sense of a whimper, and a tight, unhappy ball within him. She would be surly for days, unless he made it up to her somehow. A process she would probably seek to stretch out to the maximum benefit to herself, once she regained her tone of mind. Minds. Apology-gifts to a nonmaterial person took some ingenuity.

Assuming they survived. Well…assuming he survived.

I do not wish to end up in an ugly engineer, she whined. *Or a dolphin.*

I don't think he's ugly. Sawed-off and tough-looking, sure. Pen chose not to look down to try to spot dolphins frolicking in the distant waters.

Ikos set about hauling on one pulley-rope after another, in some balanced pattern known only to himself. The swaying jerks of the girth at each yank did unpleasant things to Pen's stomach. But, slowly and methodically, they began inching upward.

As they passed the window above Madame Gardiki's room, Pen held his breath, but no awakening dedicats or acolytes tripped over to look through and take in the sunrise. And the manrise. He could do things to disable their alarm cries like the Xarre mastiffs, but if it seemed an offense to him, it was possible the goddess would think so as well.

At least, Pen consoled himself, he had spared Madame Gardiki this ordeal. Unless she would have enjoyed it. From their few minutes of acquaintance, it was hard to know. She might have liked the part about seeing her elder son hard at work, and cleverly. Pen was pretty sure she wouldn't have liked his risks.

Pen rotated toward the sea view, watching the thin red line of light start to glow behind the Cedonian mainland, eating up the steel gray. On any other occasion, the return of the sun would be a delight. Pen longed for an eclipse. The new moon was in the wrong place for it, alas.

The vertical progression lurched to a halt just under the balconies, and Ikos commenced a complicated dance with his pulleys of tightening three lines so as to loosen and ease the one in the rear from its joist, unhook and extend it forward, rehook it, and repeat. They moved north in the thinning shadows at an excruciating pace. Ikos, above him, was breathing heavily and sweating. Pen tried to estimate the distance and time left to make the end of the row, racing the advent of the sun like very anxious, very careful slugs.

The gaolers with breakfast would be a good long stretch getting through the door. First would come time wasted trying to extract the broken key, initially seeming an annoyance rather than an emergency, then more in futile attempts to unstick the lock. Some running back and forth to find the tools for the job, and wake the women in charge of them. The hinges had been on the inside, inaccessible, or he'd have rusted them as well. The planks were thick oak, which were going to need that ax. Or a battering ram. Only once they'd broken through could they know their prisoner was missing—or suicided—and set up a cry. The echoes of woodchopping would be Pen's sign that he and Ikos had very little time left.

A red-gold sliver crested the distant hills, then became a crescent, a ball, and then too bright to look upon. The boundary of blue shadow on the slope below dropped like night's floodwaters receding. From behind the thick walls of the Order, occasional light voices echoed, too muted to make out words. In some courtyard beyond the blue roofs, a choir of several voices began a hymn, echoing and eerie with the distance. No ax-blows yet.

Ikos, just above Pen, kept grimly working. Penric, reminded of his duties as a divine and otherwise feeling to be inert cargo, began praying. There was nothing in the least rote about his morning's tally of the gods here, no.

Within Penric, Desdemona moaned. He could feel the chaos roiling within her, a growing pressure like a bad stomach about to heave up. *My demon is seasick.* The last thing in the world he needed was for her to begin vomiting unshaped disorder into the rigging that suspended them above a plummeting death. Or anywhere else nearby. He stared around like a frantic nurse looking for a bucket.

The most likely thing in sight was a trio of seagulls, rising with the morning breeze and cruising the balconies for scraps. He wondered if the ladies of the Order ever amused themselves throwing tidbits to them to be caught in midair. The pale scavenger birds were shore pests, considered sacred to the Bastard as the only god who would have them. Bastard's vermin were always allowable sacrifices.

All right, Des, Pen thought in some exasperation. *You may have one seagull. Just one.*

A burst of gratitude and chaos caught a bird on the wing as it swooped above the balcony under which they were making their transit. With a loud pop, it exploded in a shower of feathers, blood and bones turning to dust as they fell in the white flutter. Pen winced.

That was a lot of chaos. Des must have really been in distress. *Feel better now?*

The response, had it been aloud, would have approximated the hostile noise one would expect from a friend bent over a ship's rail who'd just delivered an offering to the sea.

Ikos stared up through the gaps in the boards with a disconcerted expression, but any exclamation was caught by strong teeth biting his lip.

From inside the open door to the balcony, a startled female voice said, "What?"

Another more distant voice called, "Hekat, are you coming?"

"I'll catch up in a moment. You go on ahead."

The sound of a door closing. Pen and Ikos both froze as footsteps rapped out onto the balcony boards.

Pen caught sight of the blue tunic and skirt of an acolyte as the woman bent over to pick up a few blown feathers and roll them in her fingers. She looked up. She looked down.

Both men peered back through the board-gaps. Ikos tried a friendly smile. It just made him look like a bandit delighted with the prospect of cutting a throat.

Middle-aged acolyte. How many women named Hekat could there be in this order? Dozens, for all Pen know. She wasn't an albino. But there might, unless he was fooling himself, be a faint echo of her brother in the fine frame of her face, much the way Ikos's more robust bones echoed Nikys's. Pen feared to attempt the delicate seizure of her vocal cords with Des in such disarray. As she opened her mouth to cry out, he was driven to take a different chance.

He tapped his lips twice, looked up into the brown eye he could see, and said clearly, "Surakos."

Slowly, the mouth closed, though the stare intensified.

Ikos swiveled his head and glared at Pen in complete mystification. Pen held up a hand begging silence.

"*What*," she breathed, "has Sura to do with *this*?" A wave of her hand encompassed the lunatic configuration of tackle and men hanging from her balcony joists.

"It would take about an hour to explain in full." Which they surely did not have. "But I promise you, when he comes out for your birthday in the autumn, he'll tell you everything. It should be safe for him to speak by then."

There. The birthday visit was personal information that no one who did not know Bosha could be privy to. Would it be coin enough to buy her trust?

"Why is it unsafe now?"

At least he had her attention focused on her brother, and not on the intruders' blasphemy. "Thasalon court politics."

That eye-scrunch might be a wince. "Oh, gods," she said, in a voice of loathing. "Not again."

"He'll be all right if you say nothing of what you've just seen. Except to the Lady of Spring. You can pray to your goddess. She might even speak for us."

Now the eye grew indignant. "Do you expect me to believe you have some sort of, of holy dispensation for this?"

Pen knew they did, or at least Nikys had, but it seemed unwise to test the gods. Or the acolyte. "I make no claims. Sura can tell all."

She sat with a thump, fingering her handful of feathers. "He'd better," she muttered, and Pen knew they were safe. He motioned for Ikos to continue.

Ikos shot him a hot look that suggested Surakos wasn't the only one who would be interrogated later. But he started working his pulleys and hooks again, and they recommenced their onward lurch.

Acolyte Hekat went to the gap between her balcony and the next—and last, thankfully—and hung her head over to watch their progress. "That's the most bizarre thing I've ever seen. What in the world is it in aid of?"

"Right now, removing two men from a place they should not be as expeditiously as possible. With our heartfelt apologies, I assure you."

"Were you looking at that seagull?"

"What seagull?" Pen produced an innocent blink.

She sucked breath through her teeth and gave him a gimlet glower reminding him of how the Jurald Court cook used to successfully squeeze confessions out of him about the missing pastries. Followed by a cuff to his ear and, usually, another pastry to eat on his exit. "Is Sura going to explain that, too?"

"If I get another opportunity to see him, I'll make sure he can," Pen promised.

When they swayed out of her view, she was still sitting cross-legged rolling the feathers in her hand.

Pen discovered Ikos's plan for descending from the balcony end to the stairs when they arrived, and it was even more horrifying than he would have guessed. It consisted of Ikos lengthening Pen's suspension rope and setting him in motion like a pendulum, *swinging* some twenty or more feet over to where the rising steps curved out of sight to their pilgrim-gate. "It's perfectly safe," the bridgebuilder asserted in a whisper. "Just don't get out of your girth till you've found your feet. If you slip before then, we just try again."

Pen managed his landing on the third attempt. Desdemona, crying, insisted she wanted another seagull, but he held her off.

There followed a heart-stopping interlude watching Ikos twist himself around under the balcony, fiddle with ropes, and loosen all four hooks of his evil contraption. Pen had to detach his girth and clip its doubled line to a mysterious eye-bolt in the rock face, which held it taut for Ikos as he slid down with his machine in tow. An unclipping and undoing, a rapid winding-up of rope around the engineer's arm, and the loosed end cleared its joist and fell, leaving nothing at all in its wake. Ikos somehow drew the eyebolt anchor out of its socket in three pieces, leaving only an anonymous square hole. Pen couldn't quite see if there were any other such holes pocking the rockface.

Then another maddening delay while Ikos sat down and carefully wound and folded it all into a tight, heavy bundle, no trailing ends. Pen supposed it was how he'd packed the thing up here. In the dark, all last night. Pen really wanted to take it away from him and just heave it into the sea, but Ruchia, managing to get her one-twelfth voice heard through the general cacophony that was the upset Des, agreed it would be better to leave no evidences at all. As Ikos had already concluded, apparently.

Ikos made a final survey of the balconies, and frowned aside at Penric. "Wordy bastard, aren't you?"

In so many ways. "It's my stock-in-trade."

"I'll be wanting to hear more about that, later."

"I hope you'll get a chance."

Pen reflected on all that the weary Ikos had done, starting last night at dusk. And for weeks beforehand, it seemed. All that patient labor, and no pleased mother to show for it at the end after all. He regarded the start of the two thousand steps, and murmured, "Would you like me to carry that pack?"

Ikos huffed, thick eyebrows rising in surprise at him. "Aye."

Two pilgrims on the steps. It would be no unusual thing to see (and mock, probably) and their details would be indistinguishable from a distance. Pen felt very penitential indeed as he hoisted the contraption, which turned out to weigh about thirty pounds mostly in coiled rope, on his back. As he started down in front of Ikos, he could finally hear the faint crunch of ax-blows leaking from one far window.

A last look up before the rising stone eclipsed her found Acolyte Hekat still leaning on her railing, looking down studying them. He made the tally of the gods broadly over his chest at her, tapping his lips twice by way of farewell.

She touched her fingers to her forehead in return salute, and Pen thought her brother might not be the only member of her family with a strong ironic streak.

XIV

CLOSE TO AKYLAXIO, Master Bosha found another sheltered spot to conceal the cart, where they lay up to wait out the dawn. The stop afforded more an uncomfortable doze than a sleep; still, better than nothing. His timing was good, Nikys thought, for they entered the city gates at the dewy hour when the guards were busy overseeing the influx of country folk bringing food and goods to the day-markets. Their tense wait to pass within was recompensed by being cloaked in the crowd.

The guards did not yet seem to be scrutinizing middle-aged women. If things had gone as Penric had planned, Idrene might only just now have been discovered missing on Limnos.

It didn't seem wise to assume all had gone as planned.

Still, there had to be a minimum and a maximum. If the escape was discovered at breakfast, a certain amount of time would first be spent searching the Order's precincts, and then the island. Any alarm would have the same watery barrier to pass that they had. Minister Methani's women gaolers might have to send to their master in Thasalon for instructions, though Nikys expected they'd delay that in the hopes that their report could include the prisoner being found. The period for any pursuit reaching Akylaxio could stretch out for days.

The minimum was all Nikys must worry about. If Pen had been seized last night, a military courier could have docked at Guza bare hours behind them. Although such a message couldn't have overtaken them yet, or their reception at the city gates would have been very different. If Pen had been captured... she really wasn't sure if she should be worrying for Pen, or for Limnos. But even sorcerers couldn't fly out a window, or across a strait.

The cries of gulls and the smell of the shore announced the harbor, and Nikys stretched her neck to take it in. Bigger and busier than little Guza,

smaller than Patos, much less than the maze of docks
and warehouses and forests of masts that crowded
great Thasalon's entrepot. Two piers in deep-enough
water allowed direct loading and unloading of vessels, and men and cranes were already noisily doing so
for the handful of ships tied up. The port was active
enough to rate full-time bureaucratic customs officers,
although they inspected mainly for contraband and
tax evaders. But they would also keep both provincial
and imperial lists of wanted fugitives and criminals.

Bosha, Nikys gathered, was only slightly more
familiar with Akylaxio than she was, but he found
a clean-looking inn close to the harbor, and, playing servant, escorted both women inside to secure
a room in which to rest and hide. He carried up
their luggage, not speaking until the door closed
behind them.

"I'll find a place to put up the horse and cart,"
he said, "then reconnoiter the harbor. I brought
papers that we can finish filling out when I've
found a ship." He took a sheaf from his tunic and
laid it on the washstand. "Think of what names and
personas you want to travel under. Don't leave the
room till I get back. I'll send up a maid to see about
food and drink."

"Thank you, Master Bosha," said Idrene formally, by way of accepting this program, and he nodded and departed.

Nikys went over and peeked out the window, which gave onto the other roofs of the town, mostly flat and filled with drying laundry, pots of herbs, and other useful implements. She picked up and examined the papers, which already bore seals and signatures...some of Lady Xarre's wealth was in shipping, yes, so these probably weren't even forged, wholly. Although she didn't doubt such skills were also in Bosha's repertoire, at need.

Nikys and Idrene took the chance to wash, eat, and, both familiar with the challenges of the army baggage train, reorganize their meager belongings for a quick removal when the order came. A cat-nap would be due after, to make up for the prior night.

Idrene examined Pen's medical case with interest. "This seems well thought-out. I can believe he really is a physician."

"In all but final oath. And you're snooping, Mother."

"Of course." She held up Pen's braids, which she'd unearthed in the depths, contemplating them with less irony than Bosha had. "And really a Temple sorcerer.

Not hedge. Hedge would be too risky. Temple is probably all right. So, you say you're courting?"

"He says he's courting me. I didn't say I was courting him." She removed the braids from her mother's grip and restored them to their place.

"I thought you wanted to remarry. That was why Adelis invited you to Patos, wasn't it? To meet eligible men? Or at least that's the tale you both told me."

"Yes, but all the men he introduced to me were army officers. I wasn't going to travel down that road again."

"Did you tell Adelis that?"

"Not…exactly. I didn't want to dishearten him. He *was* trying to help."

"And also, you won a trip to Patos," said Idrene, amused. She plunked down on the edge of the bed, patting the place beside her by way of invitation.

Ruefully, Nikys shrugged and sat. "I wasn't going to say that."

"True, though?"

"Yes," Nikys admitted. "Although after Adelis was blinded, I had quite different reasons to be grateful I was there."

"Yes…" said Idrene, her humor melting into pensiveness. "Hideous as it all was, I'm glad you were at his side. I think things would have gone much worse for him without you. Well, your Penric certainly has nothing of the camp about him. So has he actually asked you to wed him?"

"Yes."

"And you didn't agree to it? Why? Has he some hidden defect of character?"

"Not…not hidden. Just complicated. He's only loaned to the duke of Adria, but he is truly subordinate to the archdivine. He either has to go to a great deal of trouble to renegotiate his Temple oaths, or I would have to follow him to Adria. I don't want to go to Adria, for all he claims he'd teach me their tongue."

"Oh. Yes. Of course he'd have to speak Adriac. But it's not his native place, you say?"

"No, he's from the cantons, some obscure mountain town. But he trained in the Weald. He speaks Wealdean, Adriac, Cedonian, Darthacan, Ibran, Roknari, and I'm not sure what all else by now. He's a notable scholar."

Idrene took this in, thoughtfully. "It's true I had my fill of being dragged from pillar to post after my father, and later yours. As a home, the army has its drawbacks. And I should not like to shift myself to Orbas only for you to run off to live in Adria."

"Penric wants me to live in the air, like a bird, for all I can tell from what he's offered."

"Bachelor habits of mind, I daresay. Well, then, your solution is easy. Insist he stay in Orbas for you, and give you a house as a bride-gift. If he won't or can't, then bid him a fond goodbye."

"Mother! I'm not selling myself to the man!"

Her mother's voice went a touch drier. "But you shouldn't be selling yourself short, either. And if you don't like that bargain, perhaps it's not such a sticking-point after all, hm?"

"Mm." This was already shaping up to be one of *those* conversations with Idrene. Nikys was almost sorry she'd started it. *Or not.* Considering how close they'd come to never having such a chance again.

Idrene lowered her voice. "But you should know, Florina's jewelry is in a box walled under the plaster on the west side of her old writing cabinet. Because everyone knows to dig up the root cellar for such things. We'd always meant for you to have it for a second dowry, when you remarried. If ever you can return there before I do, find it and take it. Married or not!"

"Yes, Mother," said Nikys, thrown aback. Florma had owned some extraordinary pieces, she recalled, some of it preserved from her own noble dowry, some gifts from her husband as he rose in rank and wealth. At the least reckoning, there might be the value of a modest house out of them, with something left over.

"So there's another resource for you. Not any more chancy than marrying some chancy man. If I were you, I'd send your sorcerer to fetch it for you. Like a hero in a tale given a task to win his princess."

"He's not *my*—and I wouldn't want him to risk his life on a *third* trip to Cedonia!" She glared indignantly, which only made her mother smile.

"So, no Adria, but we have established Learned Penric is more valuable to you than jewels. Or a house. That's a start. What else?"

Nikys sighed, unwillingly driven to recite her next verse. "I wouldn't just be marrying him. I'd be marrying Desdemona. She's going to be inside his head always. Closer than a wife, more intimate than anything I can imagine."

Idrene shrugged. "Any number of women have to learn how to share their husbands with another. I grant most of them are not chaos demons. Sometimes it works very well, sometimes it works very badly, mostly it falls somewhere between. My experience, happily, was on the better end."

"How did you decide, when you went with Father?"

"Several long, frank talks, to start."

"And he persuaded you?"

"Oh, five gods forfend, I didn't talk with the general! What a pointless waste of breath that would have been. I talked with *Florina*." Idrene waved a hand. "It helped that Florina was the shrewd and experienced woman she was." She eyed Nikys. "So...you seem to think this demon is a person, or persons. A woman. Can she talk, then?"

"Yes, we've talked before this. But she has to use Penric's mouth to do so. With his permission. So it's not as if I could speak with her privately. He's always with her, and she's always with him. She'd be there with us in bed, too, I might point out."

"Oh, hm, yes. That does become very personal, doesn't it?" Idrene did not expand on this, to Nikys's relief. Though she added cheerily, "On the positive side, she could never give birth to heirs rival to your own children."

Nikys set her teeth.

Yet the notion did plant itself in Nikys's mind. If her dilemma was with the demon, perhaps it was with the demon she should be talking? It would, necessarily, be a council of three. Or fourteen.

But not impossible. And she'd seen Penric demolish impossibilities before.

I've spoken with a goddess. A demon cannot be more daunting.

It was the strangest thought she'd had in a week of strangeness. Like a seed putting out slow shoots, down into the earth and up to the sky. She left it in the tender darkness for now.

"So, no Adria, better than jewels, you'd have to sleep with a chaos demon. Although I must say, it sounds as if you've rubbed along with her fairly well so far. And she did heal Adelis." This news, apparently, had gone a long way toward reconciling Idrene to Penric's uncanny aspects.

"She and Pen together. They seem to work as a yoked pair on that sort of thing."

"An astonishing one, if so. Anything else?"

Nikys looked away. This far into her heart's fears, she might as well unburden herself of the whole basket. "You know Kymis and I were never able to get a child. I keep wondering if that was my fault... I could be condemning Pen to childlessness."

The puff through Idrene's nose held a sad familiarity. "I imagine Florma could have given you the best counsel on that. It's no small worry, I know.

But it seems to me you have its solution already. As a physician, couldn't your Penric determine the true cause? The Temple rations out its mage-physicians like water in the desert, but you hold this one in your hand."

"Mother!" Nikys flushed. "I can't ask the man to, to look up my private parts!"

"Why not? I don't imagine he'd object. As either physician or man. What, you mean you haven't tried him out in bed yet? I would have, in your place."

"Yes, Drema, we know," sighed Nikys. "And I'm sure Ikos thanks you for it." She nudged her mother in fond exasperation. "I'm not sure I'd have your courage. Or whatever it was that carried you through. Bloody-minded determination."

Idrene chuckled. "Ikos has grown into such a dear man. So that worked out well in the end. It was rough along the way in parts, but of all my many regrets, Ikos was never one. Look at it this way. Either your fears are justified, in which case you run no risk, or they are not, and so they are settled in your favor. Or do you judge Learned Penric would run away at the news he was to be a father?"

"...No. Absolutely not. He may even have it in his mind."

"Another thing you haven't talked about with him? This list is getting long, dear Nikys."

She hunched. "I'd be betting my whole life on the man. I did that once with Kymis. And then he went and *died* on me." The furious helplessness of that loss still reverberated, when she made the mistake of remembering.

"Oh." Idrene's smile grew crooked. "I know the answer for that one. It worked quite well for Florina. And your father. And Ikos's father, too."

Nikys raised her face. "You do? What?"

She tapped Nikys's forehead in a gesture not quite a blessing. And said, in a voice as arid as Nikys had ever heard from her, "Die first."

XV

S THE SUN climbed, Penric and Ikos descended, negotiating the narrowest passages of the pilgrim stairs, scarcely wider than Pen's aching shoulders, to where they widened out. The elevation was much reduced by this point. Desdemona had calmed somewhat. So Pen finally asked her, *Grant you the machine was strange, and I know you've never liked heights, but why the extreme fear, Des?*

It was an extreme drop.

You couldn't have died no matter what went wrong.

A reluctant hesitation. *Sugane died from a fall.*

Des's very first human rider had been a Cedonian mountain woman of the northern peninsula. Pen still had to work to keep her broad country accent from leaking into his Cedonian, although he'd smoothed it out quite a bit through listening to Nikys's and Adelis's Thasalon-trained voices.

A day or so after, Des went on. *She was brought to Litikone's house, which was how I came to jump to her. It's not a memory I've shared with you. It wouldn't help you.*

Des tended to keep that final part of all her riders' histories not secret, Pen thought, so much as private. *Do you think your chaos might have contributed to the accident? You wouldn't have had it under such good control back then.*

A shifty pause. *Might have. It was almost two centuries ago. Even demons forget.*

Not much, in Pen's observation. But even demons mourned, and had a long time to do so. Grief, guilt, regret...not everything they learned how to do from their human riders was a boon. He did not press.

Ikos called a halt where the stairs twisted back to become more of a trail through scree, zig-zagging down leftward toward what Pen thought might be a boat landing. He could glimpse a timber dock, but no boats, set in a ragged bite of shoreline that could barely be called a cove.

"I'll have my pack, now," said Ikos, holding out a hand.

Pen's legs were quivering custard and his mouth was dry, but he offered gamely, "I could haul it a bit farther. Where are we going?"

"I'm going to my boat." Ikos gestured right to where a faint path led away to some hidden track above the water.

Yes, of course Ikos, with his meticulous planning, would have a boat waiting to take his mother off the island. Unlike Pen, whose plans had been more nebulous at this point, involving blending with departing pilgrims.

"You can go anywhere else you please." Standing a couple of steps above Pen, Ikos could frown down at him. "Sorcerer."

"Ah, hm. When did you figure that out?"

"Candles don't light themselves. Seagulls don't burst in midair, no matter what crap they've been eating. And I still don't know what kind of spell you cast on that poor acolyte, but I want no parts of it. I know sorcerers leak bad luck, and I don't want yours anywhere near a boat I'm on."

"I didn't put any kind of a geas on Acolyte Hekat!" Pen protested. Not that he had a way of proving it to Ikos. There were good reasons sorcerers learned to be discreet. "And I'm not a hedge sorcerer. I'm Temple-trained. Learned Penric kin Jurald, formerly of Martensbridge, sworn divine of the Bastard's Order." And of the white god in Person, but that was another story. He left off his younger-brother courtesy title of *Lord*, as he usually did, since Ikos seemed a man who would not be impressed by such empty baubles. Pen had come far from Jurald Court, tucked in its valley in the distant cantons.

In so many ways, murmured Des.

"Formerly of Martensbridge? Wherever that is," said Ikos skeptically. "Where're you from now?"

"That's unsettled at present. I'm waiting for Nikys to decide. If she says yes, probably Orbas, for the time being. If no…I don't know."

Ikos's face screwed up. "Why hasn't she said yes? Widow 'n all."

"I wish I knew," Pen sighed, ignoring Des's *Do you want a list?* "I'm working on her. And not with magic, I might point out. Self-evidently."

"Hm…"

"The point is, I promise I can keep my demon's chaos off your boat. It might be hard on a passing seagull. Or a shark, or whatever. But I'm certainly

not going to befoul or sink a ship I'm sailing in!"
He added, prudentially, "Though neither sorcerers
nor gods have any control over the weather."

Ikos folded his arms. "I've got no reason to trust
anything you've said is true."

"I trust you." *More or less.* "I rode in your evil
device. Isn't that proof enough?"

"It was perfectly safe!" snapped Ikos. "You're
here, aren't you?"

"So is my magic. You're here, aren't you?"

Ikos's head went back and his lips tightened, but
he did not at once reply.

"Look." Pen scratched his hot and sticky scalp.
His fingers came away darkened. "How do you
decide anything is sound? You test it, don't you?"

"If I'm trying out new gear," said Ikos, "I usually test it to destruction. To be sure."

"Ah. If you had two sorcerers, you could try
that, I suppose. You see the problem."

Ikos snorted.

"I was thinking more along the lines of a
question." *Ask me anything* seemed a dangerously
open-ended invitation, so Pen left it at that.

"Doesn't work too well if I'm trying to decide
whether you're telling the truth in the first place,"

Ikos pointed out. "But, I don't know... What's Nikys's objection to you? You being a learned divine and all. Seems to me the sort of thing women ought to like." His lips tweaked up. "No complaining you come home from work all smelly, eh?"

Pen suspected that had not been a compliment. "I can't say," he replied, if not with truth then with precision. "But when Nikys received the letter reporting her mother had been arrested and taken to Limnos, I was the first person she came to for help. If you don't trust me, could you trust her?"

Ikos considered. Or wavered. Or at any rate, thought about it. "I like the girl," he said at last. "Pretty solid."

"I know."

"Huh."

"You have a boat, and I urgently need to get to Akylaxio. I could pay for your time and trouble." Pen did not suggest a price; no need for anyone to know how much of Duke Jurgo's purse he was still carrying.

"Not my boat. It belongs to some friends."

"All right, I could pay them."

Ikos pursed his lips. "Doubt they'll like to have a sorcerer aboard, either."

"You don't have to mention my calling. Or anything else about me, really."

"You want me to lie to my friends?"

"You want to listen to this same argument all over again, at length? If you think you're tired of it, imagine how I feel. You don't have to lie. Just… leave it out."

"Which tells me something about you, I suppose." Nothing that Ikos approved of, by the sardonic expression on his sweaty copper face.

Pen waved his hands in frustration. "I'm supposed to meet your mother and Nikys in Akylaxio, to escort them on to Orbas. It could be a chance for you to see them. Your last for a while."

"Oh." A pause. "Why didn't you say so first?"

While Pen was still mentally flailing for a reply, Ikos led off down the side path. "Come on, then," he said over his shoulder. A tight smile. "You can carry the machine."

PEN SCRAMBLED after his guide for about two miles on the scrubby trail following the shoreline. In a tiny cove, they found the boat attended by three men as sunbaked and tough-looking as Ikos. The crew waved and exchanged laconic greetings with him, but stared at Pen.

"That your mother, is it?" said one. "There's things you haven't told us about your family, Ikos, my lad."

Ikos shrugged. "Change of plans. It seems my mother's gone to Akylaxio. We need to get there."

"What, after all your trouble?"

"Aye. I'm not best pleased about it either." He jerked a thumb over his shoulder. "This one says he'll pay for the ride."

The dickering was short, since Pen, wildly anxious to be gone, closed the deal at the first suggested price. The fellows, who could have been brothers to the hardy fishermen Pen had observed putting out from Guza, presumably had been told by Ikos what risks they ran, or if not, it wasn't for Pen to apprise them.

Riding in the clear water as if floating on air, the boat might well be just such a day-fishing vessel, smelling of sun-warmed tar and timber, salt and fish-scales. It would have been substantial for the cold lakes of the cantons, but seemed disturbingly undersized for this vast blue sea. When they cast off

and raised its one sail, Pen hunkered up in the shift-
ing shade and left its management to the men who,
he hoped, knew what they were doing. Ikos doubtless thought it was perfectly safe, because he curled
up on a folded sack and fell into a doze. Either that
or he was just too exhausted to care.

Had Nikys and Idrene reached Akylaxio
unharmed? Or had they run afoul of some trouble or delay in that long night-ride they'd planned
up the coast road? Lamed horse, cart-wheel come
off, a tumble into a ditch? Or bandits? Pen expected
Bosha could speedily dispose of one bandit, or two,
but what if there'd been, say, six, or a dozen?

*Two ex-army widows are not going to make for
easy victims,* Des pointed out. *I doubt Bosha would
end up doing all the work himself.*

That was not quite reassuring. Although Pen
was subtly impressed with what little he'd seen
of Idrene's cool head so far. And Ikos, who knew
her better, had plainly believed she'd handle his
vile machine without panicking. Or puking. (Des
growled.) If it was true that women turned into
their mothers as they aged, Pen's future with Nikys
might prove even better than he'd hoped.

If they both lived to see it. Or even start it.

The women couldn't yet have been overtaken by official pursuit, more dangerous than bandits, he persuaded himself. At this hour, Idrene's gaolers should still be searching Limnos. As the boat tacked southward to parallel the coast, he leaned up to watch as the island fell behind them.

And so he was the first to spot the slim, speedy patrol galley, ten oars on a side and sail set as well, as it rounded Limnos's rocky, surf-splashed curve. No fishing or cargo vessel, that. It reeked of military purpose. A distant figure in its prow pointed an arm at them and shouted something, and the galley began to angle in their direction.

Pen crept over and shook Ikos by the shoulder. "We seem to have company. Might be trouble."

Ikos stood up on his knees by the thwart, scowled, and swore.

I could take care of them if you wanted, Des suggested. *Just like pirates.* An unsettling sense of the chaos demon licking her nonexistent lips. *Ripped sails. Snapped stays. Fouled oars. Popped pegs. Opened seams in the hull. Fires in the galley. So many amusing things to be done...*

No wonder captains didn't want sorcerers aboard.

Ruchia was the only part of Des to protest. *Stay calm. If they've anything to do with us, they are looking for an escaped woman. No women on this boat. Let them search, and then go away.*

Yes, Pen agreed with Ruchia. He offered a sop. *And should things go badly, there might be an opportunity later for even* more *chaos.*

Not at all fooled, Des gave way, grumbling.

Ikos's crewmates didn't look any happier than he did at this visitor. Pen had heard that Cedonian islanders sometimes supplemented fishing with less benign sources of income. Smuggling. Or even piracy. But—he glanced around their lightly laden vessel—they didn't seem to be carrying any obvious contraband today.

And no escaped prisoners, either.

"Where did that thing come from?" Pen asked Ikos. The galley looked all-business, and they clearly stood no chance of outrunning it in this mild weather.

"Imperial navy keeps a station around the other side of the island," Ikos replied. "Not a full garrison. Couriers, mainly, and vessels to carry the alarm to the mainland if a threat should heave over the horizon." He added after a moment, "I checked. Didn't you?"

Pen let that poke pass.

When the galley drew close enough for shouts of
Heave-to! to carry across the water, Ikos's crew reluctantly did so. Oars were raised, and some officers
clustered at the rail, looking down into their open
boat. A young sailor in an imperial uniform climbed
along a rope net and made a daring leap aboard.

"We're searching for a woman." He gave a brief,
tolerably accurate description of Idrene. His first
close look around verified there was no one of that
sex aboard, although he stared hard at Pen, distracted for a moment by his foreign eyes. Which
were not the brown of his quarry, so he went on,
"She might be drowned by this time. If you find
her body, bring it to the officers at the Limnos cove.
There's a reward. Pass the word."

Ikos's crew mumbled some interest in that last,
and the sailor caught the rope tossed from his galley
and managed the harder trick of returning upward,
without even dipping himself in the waves. Ikos
pushed off with one of their own oars, and, as soon
as they were clear, the galley's oar bank came down
and bit the water once more. Going who-knew-
where, but, as Ruchia had predicted, *away.*

And not ahead of them toward Akylaxio, or at
least, not yet.

Penric exhaled and sat, bonelessly.

Ikos sank down beside him. Judging by his wheezing, Pen was not the only one with his heart thumping in his ears.

"Word will reach the mainland by nightfall, then," said Ikos.

"Yes. Although word of what is an open question. It looks as though they bit on my suicide lure, at least in part." But not conclusively. Still, the pursuers would have to search everywhere, and Idrene and Nikys were in just one place. Would they imagine Idrene had fled inland, or realize that she sought a ship?

"If m'mother had been aboard with me just now," Ikos observed after a distant minute, "that would not have gone well."

"Quite," agreed Pen. "I plan to dedicate a hymn to the white god, when I get a chance to breathe."

Ikos cocked his head. "The Bastard your god, too?" And answered his own question, "Yes, of course, must be. If you're His divine. So, having His ear, so to speak, can you ask Him to bless this voyage?"

Pen gestured the tally of the gods, and tapped his lips twice with his thumb. "By every sign," he said, "He already has."

"...Aye."

They sat together in reflective silence as the boat tacked south.

XVI

NIKYS SNAPPED AWAKE at a rap on the chamber door, her sleep-slurry washed away by alarm. Thankfully, it was Bosha. She snared a quick look out the window to check the time as Idrene sat up on the edge of the bed, yawning, and Bosha took off his hat and settled on a stool. Late afternoon; they'd slept a good stretch. Perhaps two more hours till sunset?

"What did you find?" asked Idrene.

Bosha grimaced. "Nothing good yet. Of the ships now at dock, three are headed the wrong way, one is not suitable for unescorted women, and the last is a Xarre-owned vessel. You will understand if I'd prefer not to place you there, but in any case, its next port of call is Thasalon, which you'd best avoid."

Idrene nodded. Nikys couldn't decide whether to be worried or relieved. Sooner away was better, but a delay might allow Penric to catch up with them. …If nothing awful had befallen him.

"How long, do you think," said Idrene, "should we wait for a better chance before giving up and heading east overland? Could you drive us to a coach road?"

"Maybe," said Bosha, obviously not liking this much better than putting them on a Xarre ship. "But your description will certainly reach any border before you. This whole scheme depends on speed."

Indeed, outrunning pursuit was all their hope. Resisting it, should it catch them, was out of the question without Penric, and even more terrifying to contemplate with him.

"Three ships are putting out on this tide," said Bosha. "I'm told Akylaxio gets half-a-dozen seagoing merchanters a day docking to load or offload. A couple of day-coasters call regularly"—local ships that passed to and from the smaller towns and islands—"but that's not a first choice."

Not a good choice at all. They would repeat the same risks at every port, and accumulate delays.

Idrene rubbed her sleep-creased cheeks. "Let's give it till tomorrow morning to see what else arrives. Then take counsel and decide." She rose to splash her face at the basin, and went to peer out the window. "I confess, I'm growing mortally tired of being trapped in small rooms."

Bosha gave her a sympathetic nod, and with the women's collaboration turned to filling out as much of their documents as he could. It seemed he could alter his handwriting at will, Nikys noticed. He put down his quill and looked up at a fresh tap on the chamber door. "That may be dinner." He rose to open it, though his other hand hovered on the hilt at his belt.

But it wasn't the maidservant who stumbled through. It was Penric. And...

"Ikos!" Idrene shrieked, dashing across the room and falling upon him.

He seized her back, huffing relief. "So it was all true...!"

"Keep your voices down," Penric and Bosha chorused.

Bosha glanced at this new man and opened his hand in pressing query to Penric, who shrugged and closed the door firmly behind them. "Brother," he muttered. "The other brother."

"Oh. The bridgebuilder? But what...?"

"He was a surprise to me, too."

Penric was altered in coloration yet again, his hair now a sandy brown, sticky with salt, and his head and arms and feet paler, but mottled, like a peculiar tan or a mild skin disorder. He was back in his tunic and trousers, noticeably grubbier.

Ikos looked, and smelled, as if he were home from a very bad, very long day at work, stubbled and sunburned, clothes crusty with dried sweat. Nikys hugged him anyway. Pen looked on as if...envious? Breaking away from Ikos because Idrene was elbowing in again, Nikys's fingers stretched and closed. She didn't need her hands to assure herself of Pen's reality; her eyes were enough, in this company. For a moment she wished her company anywhere but here.

Idrene's anxious questions tumbled over one another. "What are you doing here, you shouldn't be within a hundred miles of me, whatever are you two doing together, how did you *get* here?"

"Fishing boat," said Ikos, choosing the simplest from this spate. "From Limnos."

"I was worried how we'd get into Akylaxio discreetly," Penric put in, "but it turns out that a brace of those big tuna fish make an excuse to dock at any harbor, no questions asked. We picked them up along the way. Ye *gods*, they're huge in a small boat. For a moment I thought they'd sink us. I'd only seen them laid out flat in the markets at Lodi, before."

"You stopped to go fishing?" said Idrene, sounding bewildered.

"No," said Ikos distantly, "we didn't stop. They leaped into the boat all on their own, and died at our feet. Smiling. Apparently."

That...ah, that wasn't a joke. Or sarcasm. Nikys had seen that round-eyed look on people before, and what did it say that she recognized it? He wasn't poleaxed, just Penric'd. Her lips stretched up unwilled.

"We left the lads to sell the fish," Ikos went on, "and strolled around at random till he found you."

"It wasn't random," Pen protested, "it was logic. Mostly. But tell me everything that's happened to you!"

They ended up with Idrene and Nikys seated on the edge of the bed, Penric on the stool, and Ikos at Idrene's feet, her hand fondling his hair, urgently swapping tales. Bosha leaned silently against the wall with his arms folded, taking in, Nikys thought, everything, although even his set face screwed up with consternation at parts. He did not look best pleased when he learned about the encounter with his sister Hekat, nor Pen's promise that her brother would tell her all about it on his next visit. "All that seems safe," Pen temporized, which did not improve matters.

Bosha broke off to answer the door and receive the dinner tray from the maid, and order more food, very necessary as the two men fell upon the offering like starved wolves.

The second round of dinner was delivered and consumed before they came to the end of Penric's and Ikos's intertwined and often clashing explanations, frequently dislocated by Idrene's many questions. "You do make me wish I'd been able to ride in your machine," Idrene told Ikos. "It sounds splendid. Perhaps, at some happier time, you might get a chance to demonstrate it for me." Ikos smiled. Penric rubbed his jaw, squeezing some remark to unintelligibility.

Nikys left out from her account only her strange experience in the court of the sacred well, and Pen did not press her on it, to her silent gratitude. She turned at last to Ikos.

"But you say you have a boat?"

He shook his head. "Not my boat, and nothing that could take you to Orbas."

Pen scratched his scalp and grimaced. "I'm thinking I want to find a bathhouse before I board anything. I'll circle back through the harbor and see what's come in since the last check, after."

Idrene was clearly torn between sending Ikos with him, or keeping her son at her side for every possible moment before they had to part. But Ikos stretched, his joints making disturbing muffled crunching noises, sniffed his armpit without prompting, and chose to depart with Penric.

Nikys fell backward on the bed, floating between elation and new terror. The latter hardly seemed fair. Given how she'd fretted at Penric's absence, surely his presence should be the cure? Perhaps this was what a gambler felt when he laid his whole stake on one last throw of the dice. Not a thrill she relished, it seemed.

IT WAS nearly dark, Nikys was anxious, Idrene was pacing from wall to wall, and Bosha was staying out of her way, when the two men returned, much cleaner.

And triumphant. Penric barely closed the door behind him before he blurted, "Two more ships have docked. One is Roknari—"

A general flinch.

"—but the other is Saonese. Heading homeward, near full-laden. It's not going to Orbas, but it is planning a stop at the Carpagamon islands, and from there it should be no challenge to double back to the duchy."

"Do you speak Saonese?" asked Nikys. A difficult dialect of Darthacan; she had a working command of the latter.

"Oh, yes, it's practically my father-tongue. Jurald is a Saonese name, you know. And there was Learned Amberein, one of Des's riders before me. The purser thought I was an expatriate fellow-countryman. I didn't correct him. Time for that later. Anyway, they keep a few cabins aboard for independent merchants transshipping cargo. Only one free, but I booked it. More space than a coach, at least. Another may open up later in the voyage. They sail on the morning tide."

"Should we go there now?" asked Idrene, looking ready to dive for their baggage.

Pen shook his head. "The Customs shed closes at dark. We're supposed to board in the morning."

Bosha drummed his pale fingers on his thigh. "That could be cutting things fine."

"Yes." Pen bit his lip. "Though it would be the usual course for passengers."

"Mm," said Bosha. There seemed no choice but to accept this delay. Nikys wondered if she'd sleep at all tonight.

Pen had secured a chamber across the hall for the two men and Bosha, though Ikos lingered with Idrene and Nikys. He'd been supposed to be at his next worksite two weeks ago, although he claimed his crew could begin surveying without him. They would say their goodbyes indoors in private tomorrow; he planned to watch over their departure from a distance with Bosha till they were safely away.

They talked in low tones until his head was nodding, and his mother sent him to bed with a kiss the like of which he'd probably not had from her since he was four. It seemed to please them both. It often felt to Nikys that her elder brother's relationship with their mother was less, not more, complicated than her own for its long gap, but she could not begrudge it.

XVII

$\mathcal{P}$EN FOLLOWED HIS fellows into the women's chamber at dawn, for breakfast and for Bosha to put the finishing touches on their papers. There was nothing more to pack, but Nikys pulled Pen's Temple braids from his medical case and held them up in doubt.

"The customs officers may search our baggage. Is there some better way to hide these, Pen?"

Pen sighed and took them from her. "I suppose I'd better abandon them. They can be replaced when we get home." And when had he started thinking of Orbas, of all places, as home? "It's more imperative just now to conceal that I'm a Temple sorcerer than to prove I am."

The other side of Bosha's lip curled. "Give them to me for a moment." A bit reluctantly, Pen handed them over, and Bosha examined the knot holding the loops. A few moves of those deft, pale fingers, and the cord fell into one long length. "Madame Khatai, might you sit here?" He gestured to the stool.

Her eyes rolling in curiosity, Nikys sat as instructed. Bosha plucked her hairbrush from her valise and busied himself about her head. Idrene drifted over to watch. Within a few minutes, he had somehow turned her hair into a raised confection with the braids visible as no more than a few fashionable glints holding the black curls.

"Oh, that's charming!" exclaimed Idrene. Pen had to agree.

Nikys smiled, reaching up for an uncertain prod. The arrangement held firm. "Very clever, Master Bosha. Thank you!"

"Do encourage General Arisaydia in his quest for Lady Tanar's hand, Madame Khatai."

"Do you favor him for her, then?" Nikys's smile didn't alter, but Pen thought she was listening for every nuance in the answer. Because Bosha would have them. And Bosha's opinion in this affair mattered far more than was obvious.

"She's had much worse, sniffing about her." He rubbed his neck beneath his white braid. "You know, her latest interest is in going up onto the roof to learn celestial navigation. She conscripts one of Lady Xarre's captains for her lessons, when he stops in to give his reports. If she's not married to your brother, or some man of like merit, with her vast vitality diverted to children, I'm afraid she will insist on apprenticing as an officer on one of Lady Xarre's ships. And if denied, would run off to become a pirate queen."

This was *probably* a joke, Pen thought. Probably. Hard to tell with Bosha. Or with Tanar, for that matter.

Nikys dimpled. "Do pirate queens keep secretaries?"

"I dread finding out." His smile faded altogether. "Although childbed is the one place even I cannot go to defend her. Perhaps the high seas would be better after all."

Idrene said gently, "We cannot protect anyone from being alive, Master Bosha. No matter how much we might wish to." Her eyes fell on her own children.

His lips stretched in an expression Pen would hesitate to call amused. "I can try."

And then it was time for final farewells, teary when Idrene and Nikys embraced the sheepish, but gratified, Ikos. Pen stifled his jealousy. He, after all, would be the one getting to keep the women.

If I can. He hoisted the baggage and shuffled after them to the stairs.

THE BLUE Cedonian sky was hazier this morning as they walked down to the harbor. If this heralded some change in the fine weather, Pen thought, eyeing it, it wasn't going to be soon enough to impede their departure.

The squawks of white gulls played over the clatter of men and equipment on the two piers readying ships for sea. Crates of goods from last night's unlading were piled up ashore, waiting for their carriers to come take them to their inland destinations. A crew of men unpacked an arriving wagon, lifting long ceramic flasks of wine from their straw bed and carting them off to a dock. Another crew wrestled with ingots of copper, distinctive with their green patina and red scratches, stacking them on a handcart. Ikos watched it all with great professional interest, as he and the behatted Bosha, mismatched sightseers, veered off to loiter on a low wall as if enjoying the maritime spectacle.

"All this way," mourned Pen, "and I never saw great Thasalon."

"Since any view we're like to get would be from inside an imperial prison," said Idrene, "best not to make that wish."

"Aye," Pen sighed.

Idrene clutched the packet with their papers as they approached the Customs shed. Nikys raised her chin and inhaled.

At a clatter of hooves on the cobblestones behind them, Penric wheeled around. And froze.

A man in the uniform of an imperial courier dismounted from his sweating horse and tied its reins to a bollard, looking over the docks and ships with sharp, flashing eyes. Turning to his saddlebags, he withdrew a leather dispatch case. He began to walk purposefully toward the Customs shed.

"Keep smiling, don't panic, and play along," Pen muttered through his teeth to Nikys and Idrene as they paused to see what had distracted him, and stiffened in turn. "I can take care of this."

Nikys gripped Idrene's hand. In caution? In reassurance?

This one is going to be costly, warned Des, fully alert. It wasn't an attempt to dissuade him.

Not nearly as costly as failing, Pen thought grimly back.

Aye.

Sight, Des.

Pen set down their baggage and moved to intercept the courier, plastering a smile on his features. That strange, compelling, colorful interior view of a soul's essence, hidden within the outer material form, flickered into focus in Pen's mind's eye. "Oh, **officer!**" he called, the reverberations of the shamanic weirding voice entering his tones even as he pushed the words out. They touched the man like tendrils, barely catching on that firm sense of duty. His head jerked toward Pen, and he frowned, but stopped.

"Good morning," Pen continued. "Have you ridden from Guza?"

Pen felt the assent swirling within the man even as he returned in a quelling growl, "What is it to you?"

"I think **you want to let me see that paper,**" Pen purred, holding out his hand as though such an exchange were the most natural thing in the world. The fellow shook his head as if throwing off an insect, but, slowly, opened his case. **"You need to deliver that paper to me**."

The courier extracted a document, stood at some echo of attention, and held it out. Pen took it and ran his eyes hastily through what he guessed was some standard Cedonian bureaucratic preamble—Bosha would know—to the critical paragraph, a description of Idrene in much the same terms as the sailor had given them yesterday afternoon. The official detainment order for the customs inspectors, clearly.

Pen twitched it behind him and set it alight. It was a puff of ash before it reached the cobbles.

"You have delivered your urgent message to the Customs-shed officer," Pen continued, driving the words, and the geas of persuasion, as deep into his target as possible. The tendrils set like hooks, like sucking mouths, into the officer's spirit, and Pen winced. Geases could be nasty almost-organisms, at times, parasitizing the life of their victim for their own prolongation. A true shaman could create one that would last for weeks. Pen hoped for a day. **"You have done your duty. Now you need to take care of your loyal horse."** A geas worked best when laid in alignment with the subject's natural inclinations. **"And then go drink a flagon of wine. You've earned it. You delivered your message in Akylaxio just as ordered."** Pen simulated a Cedonian military salute, which the man, his eyes slightly dazed, returned.

Blinking, the man returned to his horse, untied it, and led it off. By the time he reached the street, his steps were a firm stride again. He didn't look back. He might bear other copies of the circular to deliver further along the coast, but their existence did not concern Pen.

Still sitting on the wall overlooking it all, both Bosha and Ikos swiveled their heads in worry to watch the officer. Not looking back at them, Pen managed an *it's all right, stand down* wave, which he hoped they interpreted correctly.

It wasn't entirely all right. Memory alteration fiddled not only with free will but with the very essence of a soul, and thus bordered on sacrilege. *Good intentions* and even *good results* were valid theological defenses only up to a point. Pen could hope he'd not transgressed beyond it. He wouldn't say *pray*, as he'd decided long ago not to bother the gods with questions when he didn't really want to hear the answers.

The blood was already starting to trickle. Pen snorted and sucked it back to send down his throat. "Now I need to get out of sight for a few minutes," he told the women. "Quickly."

Nikys, who had watched him with the sacred dogs, understood at once. She dropped Idrene's hand and grabbed Pen's, towing him back toward the stacks of crates as the trickle turned into a flood and Pen choked, gasped, and choked again. His eyes watered wildly. He clapped his other hand to his mouth as he coughed out blood. It stained his palm in quick stripes as he reached the shelter and dropped to his knees, then his hands and knees, coughing wetly. The scarlet splattered onto the stones, spreading.

And kept coming. Struggling for breath between spasms, Pen wondered if he could actually drown himself. There was a new hazard for the list...

"Mother's tears, Pen!" gasped Nikys, holding his quaking shoulders. "This is much worse than before."

And Idrene's startled voice, "Is he *dying*?"

It must look as if he were hacking out his lungs in gobbets. Which, admittedly, sounded much more dramatic than *It's a nosebleed*. Pen wheezed and shook his head. "Ugly magic," he got out between coughs. "High cost. Des hates it." Shamanic magics did not come naturally to a chaos demon, and Pen suspected his body paid a premium price for his use of them at all. It was as if chaos and blood were coins of two different realms, and the moneylender charged an extortionate fee for their exchange.

Should I do something? Des asked, anxious. *There are harbor rats lurking about...*

Don't. Trying to divert or delay his somatic payment for this magic with some uphill healing had unpleasant side-effects, afterward. Better than dying, to be sure, but still better was to pay off the debt at once. It just looked alarming.

He studied the cup or so of blood splashed on the ground under his face. All right, *was* alarming. But his desperate coughing ceased, his lungs stopped pulsing, and the blood issuing from his stinging nose dwindled to mere drips, then tailed off altogether. He let Nikys roll him into her arms, smiling weakly up at her distraught face.

He should explain about the nosebleed, but her lap was such a lovely soft cushion...

Malingerer, scoffed Des.

Are you going to tell on me?

Never. He knew he was going to be all right when his demon's temporary fright faded back into amusement. *Enjoy your treat. After all, so do I.*

Not thinking about that, Des. It throws me off my stride.

As you wish.

"Bastard's teeth, is all that red gush his?" asked Ikos's voice, much too close to Pen's ear.

"You were supposed to steer clear of us." Pen cracked open his eyes. "You two." Bosha had taken up a guard stance at the entry of the space between the crate stacks. Pen added to Ikos, "This, by the way, is what happens to me when I force a geas on an unwilling person. So you see I didn't cast one on Acolyte Hekat yesterday."

"Huh." His face retreated out of Pen's sight.

"Should I follow that courier and do anything about him?" Bosha asked over his shoulder in a neutral tone.

Was he offering to assassinate the man? *Dear me, he is!* crowed Des. *What a handy fellow to have around.* Pen hastened to explain that his geas made further intervention unnecessary, which Bosha, after a considering moment, accepted.

Ikos returned with what proved to be his shirt, wetted with seawater, and handed it to Pen without comment.

"Do I look a fright?"

Nikys nodded, her clutch not slackening.

"I'd best tidy up. I don't want to be kept from boarding because they fear I have some sort of plague. Aside from being a sorcerer." Deciding, since it was Ikos's shirt, that he couldn't make it much worse, Pen wiped the gore from his face and hands—he'd managed to keep most of the splash off his tunic—then let Nikys have it to finish the job to her satisfaction.

One gives you the shirt off his back, mused Des, *and the other offers to help you bury bodies. I do believe you have made some new friends, Pen!*

Hush, Pen thought back. But he believed so, too. Or a brother-in-law and a...did Idrene realize they were going to acquire a eunuch-in-law?

I imagine she will, said Des. *She seems quite as shrewd as Nikys.*

He grinned and let Ikos and Nikys pull him to his feet. The gray dizziness passed off as he caught his breath.

When he had composed himself, the three taking ship continued the interrupted trek for the Customs shed, leaving Ikos and Bosha to lurk warily among the crates. Pen let Idrene, all assured-army-widow this morning, although of a different and fictional officer, present their papers to the clerk. They all watched in feigned indifference as their baggage was turned out onto the table, but it was soon clear this modest party bore no contraband. The clerk grew interested in Pen's medical case, though not for any official reason, and seemed content with Pen's explanation that he was an aspiring student of the healing arts.

Then it was time to traverse the dock to the gangplank of the Saonese ship, and be herded up it by sailors ready to get underway. Three sturdy masts, Pen observed with approval, and even larger than the cargo vessel on which he'd traveled from Lodi to Patos not four months past, which now seemed a century ago. Making this Pen's second sea voyage ever. Would it be as life-altering as the first?

XVIII

A BENCH RAN along the taffrail at the stern of the big merchanter. After stowing their scant baggage in their cabin, they all went out and sat upon it to watch the sailors work the ship out of the harbor. Nikys contemplated the receding shore, as did Idrene. Their hands found each other, as if to assure that this one part of their lives, at least, was not lost to them. Pen leaned his head back under the wide sky and gazed up. Distant figures, no matter how carefully watched-for, grew indistinguishable, then the town became a blur on the sun-hazed coast, and then the coast, too, dropped below the horizon. They were away.

It felt to Nikys as though her body had been bound strangling-tight by wires, and one by one, each wire was being clipped off till none were left. She breathed, shook out her arms, sensed her blood move freely. Stretched her neck. Exhaled.

"Penric..." No, that wasn't right. "Desdemona. Can I talk with you?"

"Mm?" Pen turned his head. "Of course. Any time."

She stood. "Let's go to the cabin."

Pen followed her up at once, amiable if baffled.

Idrene smiled behind her hand. "Take all the time you like. I've had my fill of tiny rooms. I plan to sit right out here as much as possible, this voyage."

Nikys rolled her eyes, but said, "Thank you, Mother." And meant it.

The cabin was tiny indeed, two pairs of bunks built into the bulkheads facing each other across a narrow aisle. It did have a small, square window on the end, presently hooked open on the sight of the sea falling behind them, stirred by the ship's passage. The air was fresh and fine.

Nikys gestured Pen to one bunk, and sat on the other facing him. With his long legs, they were nearly knee to knee.

Nikys hardly knew where to begin, only that she had to begin. With a feeling of jumping into murky but deep water, she said, "Desdemona, have you ever been married before?"

She wasn't sure if it was Pen or Des responsible for his head going back and his eyebrows up, but she could mark the little changes in the tension of his face as the demon came to the fore. "By which I suppose you are asking if any of my sorceresses were married before?"

"Yes, that. During the time you were with them. I know some were widowed…"

Pen held up his fingers to keep count. Or Des held up Pen's fingers. "Of the ten, five were never married. Sugane, Rogaska, of course Mira, Umelan, and Ruchia. Vasia and Aulia were both widowed before they acquired me, and did not remarry after. Litikone, well, I was a very young demon then. With no Temple guidance, I suppose it seemed more like contracting a madness than a power. Her husband became frightened and moved out, which was why she went to Patos to end her days as a servant to Vasia. Who was the first to acquire me purposely, if still untutored.

"Aulia of Brajar was my first trained Temple divine, and what a huge difference that made, but she was already older, and widowed, and very firm of will. Which was how I came to be handed off at her death to the great physician Amberein of Saone. She was still married, with her childbearing behind her of course, but her husband, dear fellow, was already used to dealing with a strong-minded woman. I had not guessed a sorcerer could live in intimacy so well, before. Helvia was another of the same stamp.

"Ruchia...was Ruchia, my dearest rider until Pen. The first to really treat me as a partner and a person, if still unnamed. Forty years with her quite spoiled me for anything less."

Pen's hands had lowered to clasp between his knees; he looked up from them. "Six of the ten had borne children, before me. None after, of course."

"Why of course? Is it something to do with the chaos?"

Pen, yes, it was Pen now, cleared his throat. "Yes. Sorceresses who conceive suffer early miscarriages. Unless they are very knowledgeable and adept. Amberein or Helvia could certainly have brought a child to term, but they had already finished their families. Or Ruchia, but she did not choose it. Something emotionally complicated to do with herself being a foundling of the Bastard's orphanage, I gather."

Nikys pursed her lips. "What of sorcerers?"

"Um...I'm less sure. Well, no. I've heard of sorcerers who managed to get married, and have families." He added reluctantly, "Though they are more often bachelors or widowers. Or their wives leave them, because it's too much like living with a crazy man." He smiled ruefully as if inviting her to argue with this, and looked more rueful when she only nodded. "*I've* never been married," he pointed out. "Although I am trying to rectify that."

His lips twitched back, as Des said, "Feeling left out, lad?"

"Who wouldn't? Looking at..." A feeling gesture at Nikys, and a melting smile.

Nikys resisted melting. Barely. She tried to remember everything on her list. "I don't want to move to Adria."

Pen sat up. "I could transfer to Orbas, with some help from the duke. The duke pressuring his archdivine, rather. Even the Temple hierarchy must give way in the face of the sacrament of marriage. ...Usually." He added after a moment, "And if not, well, I'm in Orbas, they're in Adria, what are they going to do about it? Although I would like to be able to travel back there someday, at need." He nodded, as though the point were disposed of. Perhaps it was. Though, being Pen, he added after another moment, "I might still like to take you to visit Adria sometime. When it's not having a clash with Cedonia, but then, you're not going to be a Cedonian anymore, are you? It's really a very interesting realm."

Nikys grimaced. "I'd never have left Cedonia, if Cedonia had not betrayed Adelis. No going back now."

"Sometimes," sighed Pen, "that happens. Even without betrayal." Missing the white peaks of his distant cantons? Though Nikys was of the strong opinion that the Mother's Order in Martensbridge had betrayed him too, and first, through their nearly lethal mishandling of his healing skills. And he knew it, or he would not have near-fled that beloved home, either.

Nikys fought her way back to her points. "I want a house." Though she temporized, "Someday, at least. I realize it might not be possible right away."

"Well, so do I."

"Oh. ...Huh."

"I haven't spent the past decade perching in other people's palaces by choice, exactly. It was just easiest. Convenient to my work."

She supposed that was so. "I think you live mostly inside your own head. It hardly matters where you've put your body."

"So a house will do just fine, then." Another maddening smile.

She swallowed. "Children…"

"Those, too." He nodded. "They will go with the house. Like a cat."

"What?"

"That was Pen, not me," Des put in. "I don't know what he's thinking, either. Yes, you do."

Nikys drew breath and faced her darkest fear. Head-on, because it was time. "I may be barren. Kymis and I were never able to get a child." She didn't want to add, *And we tried*, though she supposed it was implied. She had never met a man before Pen so able to toss her like a coin between shyness and exasperation.

"Could be many different reasons for that." He glanced her up and down. Wait, why did it feel as though those blue eyes had just knifed through her? *Sorcerers, agh.* "There's nothing obviously amiss on your side, at least." *Was that all it took?* The eyes crinkled. "It might require some experimenting to be sure. I could help you with that."

Why did he sound just like Drema? If she'd been sitting next to him, she would have hit him. Perhaps she should shift across there, so she could.

She rubbed her forehead. "If I married Penric, he would be my husband. But what would you be, Desdemona? Now you are a person. Not my husband. Not my wife, either. My...my big sister?" There was a new thought, oddly warming.

"For you, sweetling," said the demon, with impressive confidence, "I can be anything you like."

She couldn't help what popped out. "Even silent in bed?"

"Yes, please," Pen interjected fervently.

Des grinned. "Yes. Although I predict you'll get over even that need in due course."

"I daresay," sighed Nikys. Considering all she'd become accustomed to so far. Ultimately, he would just become Pen. Or, *Pen!* (Or, maybe sometimes, *Des!*) He was nearly so already. "Spouses do rub each other smooth at the joints, given enough time."

Time. It did not wait for any human want, or grief, or plan. Or careful list. Nearly half her life might be behind her already. It was time to get started on the next half.

"Marry the sorcerer, dear," Des urged, "and put me out of his misery. He'll be glad you did. If he is happy, I can be happy. And so can you."

And that was just how it worked, wasn't it? Happiness handed around and around, never stopping. It wasn't something one could hoard tight like a miser. That would be like trying to hold one's breath for later.

Nikys looked up, and said firmly, "You can't shave your head."

"Wouldn't dream of it," Pen returned instantly. "Although…I can't promise I won't go bald, when I get old. Des, could you do something about that?"

"I've never tried. Not an issue that ever came up with my prior riders."

"By the time you grow bald," said Nikys, "I shall doubtless be fat and wrinkled."

"And sweet. Like a winter apple."

"More likely cranky."

"Sweetly cranky."

"Optimist."

"I think people must be, to do this." He'd slid across beside her. Just the sort of thing he would do, if she didn't keep her eye on him.

Not that keeping an eye on all that male elegance was a burden. What had been her first impression of him, back in the garden in Patos? *Ethereal*, that was it. He seemed very human to her now, flesh and blood and long, long bones. Mistakes and miracles, awkwardness and profound grace, sorrow and joy. Beautiful hands, slim-fingered and sensitive and so very skilled at so many things. A woman would have to be a witless fool to let those hands get away.

"It's still a long way home," she pointed out. By this time, her faintly breathed objections must be pure habit, because she was falling toward him all in air.

"Or maybe home is right here in arm's reach," he said. The arm in question curled around her, hugged tight. Like drawing a woman to shore.

She reached back.